SPECIAL MESSAGE TO READERS

This book is published under the auspices of

THE ULVERSCROFT FOUNDATION

(registered charity No. 264873 UK)

Established in 1972 to provide funds for research, diagnosis and treatment of eye diseases. Examples of contributions made are: —

A Children's Assessment Unit at Moorfield's Hospital, London.

•

Twin operating theatres at the Western Ophthalmic Hospital, London.

•

A Chair of Ophthalmology at the Royal Australian College of Ophthalmologists.

•

The Ulverscroft Children's Eye Unit at the Great Ormond Street Hospital For Sick Children, London.

You can help further the work of the Foundation by making a donation or leaving a legacy. Every contribution, no matter how small, is received with gratitude. Please write for details to:

**THE ULVERSCROFT FOUNDATION,
The Green, Bradgate Road, Anstey,
Leicester LE7 7FU, England.
Telephone: (0116) 236 4325**

In Australia write to:

**THE ULVERSCROFT FOUNDATION,
c/o The Royal Australian College of
Ophthalmologists,
27, Commonwealth Street, Sydney,
N.S.W. 2010.**

RIDE TO VENGEANCE

Reb Scott knew that all was not well when his brother, Luke, asked him to come to his small ranch. Luke had hinted that outlaws were on the rampage, but when Reb arrived at the ranch he found that trouble had already struck in no uncertain manner. A rope dangled from a tree and a wooden marker told the world that Luke himself had died a rustler's death. Reb vowed he would find out who was behind the hooded killers if it was the last thing he did.

*Books by Brad Hammond
in the Linford Western Library:*

GUN TRAIL TO LONGHORN

BRAD HAMMOND

◆

RIDE TO VENGEANCE

Complete and Unabridged

LINFORD
Leicester

First published in Great Britain in 1988 by
Robert Hale Limited
London

First Linford Edition
published 2001
by arrangement with
Robert Hale Limited
London

British Library CIP Data

Hammond, Brad, *1924 –*
    Ride to vengeance.—Large print ed.—
Linford western library
1. Western stories
2. Large type books
I. Title
823.9′14 [F]

ISBN 0–7089–5962–8

Published by
F. A. Thorpe (Publishing)
Anstey, Leicestershire

Set by Words & Graphics Ltd.
Anstey, Leicestershire
Printed and bound in Great Britain by
T. J. International Ltd., Padstow, Cornwall

This book is printed on acid-free paper

For Allan J. McCullough

1

The trouble started for Luke Scott at the end of a hard day's range riding. He was sitting on the front porch when he saw four riders come off the east fork of the Hartville road. Behind Scott, in the kitchen of their small ranch house, he could hear Sue going about fixing supper, and the smells of frying bacon and brewing coffee wafted out on the still air.

Scott's slate-grey eyes narrowed and a small frown built furrows between his eyes as he followed the movements of the riders. At first he thought they had missed their trail and would soon see their mistake, but when they continued towards the Box S buildings he knew they really intended a visit.

'Sue,' he called over his shoulder. 'Bring out my belt and gun.'

In a minute his wife was on the

porch beside him, her pretty face white and tense. She was a medium-sized girl, slim of waist and full of bosom and hip. She handed Scott his holstered .45 Colt and shaded her eyes against the sunset fires that lighted the west.

'Who is it, Luke?'

'Go inside, honey, and finish getting supper. Maybe it's only Dean Talbot paying a visit.'

Sue drew a quick breath and a tinge of colour came into her rounded cheeks. 'That's not fair, Luke.'

'I'm not blaming you, Sue. But Talbot takes a long time to realise he's beaten.'

He came easily to his feet, a tall man with strength in every line of his lean body, and buckled the belt about his waist. Sue stood on and he told her again to go inside.

When Sue had obeyed, Luke sat down on the weathered porch boards and watched the men come closer. Before they reached the fence he knew this wasn't Talbot and some of his riders. He had never seen these men before. He waited until they had passed under the wooden Box S symbol overhanging the open gate before coming to his feet again and putting his back to a porch post.

They were strange riders, well-armed and well-mounted. Three of them drew up while the fourth, a thin man in rolled-brim hat and dusty cowboy garb, pushed his horse to within a couple of yards of Scott. He was young, about twenty-five or so, the rancher judged. Around his own age. But there was an alert, crafty look in his bright blue eyes that Scott did not like.

'Afraid I'm not open for hiring, boys,' he said coolly. 'Just been going for a few months.'

'I'm Jim Dyke,' the rider replied. 'Thanks, we're not looking for work. At least not the kind that you're thinking about.'

He glanced over the yard and let his gaze linger on the neat ranch house. He fingered the tip of his narrow nose.

'Nice place you got here, Mr Scott.'

Scott started to speak and Dyke laughed softly. 'Sure, we know your name, Mr Scott . . . Now, listen, we've got a proposition for you.'

Scott let his eyes flicker to the three others at Dyke's back. They watched him closely, sober-faced and apparently bored at their companion's talk. He noticed that one of them was a Mexican, stoop-shouldered and hawk-beaked. He kept staring at the open door of the house and Scott hoped that Sue would not come out just now. A little chill was playing along his backbone and he tried to keep his anxiety from showing.

'What kind of proposition?' he heard himself saying.

Dyke lifted his thin nose and sniffed the air. He grinned. 'I do believe I smell fried pork,' he said.

'Supper's just over. Sorry.'

'Don't be sorry, Mr Scott. Don't be sorry! Us gents are used to riding on an empty stomach.'

4

Scott felt a tightening inside him. He knew he should ask these men in to eat, no matter what his feelings concerning them, but some stubborn streak in him refused to yield to his usually generous nature.

'I guess I should have introduced the boys,' Dyke was saying in his soft voice. 'The fat party with the beard is Yance Kibben. Don't he just look like a big, sad-faced dog!' Dyke laughed and the bearded rider scowled at his saddlehorn. 'The greaser's name is Jose Juarez,' Dyke went on. 'And as there is nobody to contradict him, we just let it go at that. The other thin joker is Bob Teal. And Bob reckons he's the fastest gun this side of the New Mex line.'

Scott's apprehension was growing and a slow anger edged his voice as he demanded as calmly as he could. 'What do you want at this ranch?'

'Mr Scott,' Dyke said, poking at his nose again, 'believe it or believe it not, but we want to help you.'

'Help me! How?' Scott's throat was dry and tight.

'You got a pretty nice herd, I take it?'

'I've got a small one. But I hope to breed it up.'

'Sure, you do. What rancher doesn't? But you've got to admit there's some boys going around with a wide loop at the end of their ropes, and they ain't too particular where they swing them.'

'There's a cattleman's protection committee,' Scott said thinly. He knew he should be ordering them off his land but there was something sinister and compelling about the bright-eyed man, and he was curious to know what was on his mind.

'There is,' Dyke agreed, nodding vigorously. 'Gents with flour sacks over their heads who ask no questions and sure like planting cottonwood fruit. But we've got a better system, and lynching has no part in it.'

Scott waited, feeling the heat draining

out of the sun and hearing a door flapping in the new breeze at the back of the house. The three had moved their horses a little and were now fanned out closely behind their leader.

'This here group you're looking at is a cattlemen's protection outfit, Mr Scott.'

'What!' Scott started to laugh but the hard intensity of Dyke's bright eyes choked it off short. 'You really mean that? But what can you do that the — '

'That the killers can't do?' Dyke said bluntly. The softness had gone from his voice and the humour from his eyes. 'You don't like that name, Mr Scott. A lot of other folks don't like it neither. A lot of folks would like to know the real names of the jokers who go around with their faces covered with flour sacks and pillow cases.'

'I know nothing about them,' Scott said harshly. 'I've got nothing to do with them.'

'Good! I'm glad to hear you say so,

Mr Scott. And this would make you all the more keen to hear what we've got to say. You know, these hooded riders always hit at nesters and small ranchers like yourself, and it looks like somebody is dead set on getting this whole range for himself.'

'I'm listening,' Scott said tersely. 'But I haven't got much more time to spare.'

'Time! Mr Scott, time just doesn't exist. It's a myth. I'm a bit of a philosopher, you know, and I've worked the whole thing out.'

'Better keep to brass tacks, Jim,' the black-bearded rider cut in sharply.

'Right, Yance! You jaspers don't appreciate me, no how. Now, Mr Scott, this is how we operate. You can go about your work and not worry about nesters and small-timers stealing your beef or running their own iron on your mavericks. You won't have no call running to the killers for help.'

'Regulators,' Scott said thinly.

'Regulators. Killers. They're all the

same to me,' Dyke said impatiently. 'They all use high trees and a hangman's knot. Now, we guarantee to keep wideloopers and thieving nesters at bay for a small payment.'

'Ah!' Scott ejaculated. 'How much?'

'A miserable hundred bucks a month,' Dyke rejoined quickly. 'Payable in advance.'

Scott threw his head back and laughed. 'It's the craziest thing I ever heard of.'

'I told you, Jim,' Yance Kibben said impatiently. 'This gent couldn't afford it.'

'You bet I couldn't,' Scott told the bearded rider. 'And even if I could, I wouldn't have anything to do with your idea.'

Dyke's blue eyes were flashing and his lean face became a cruel mask as he pushed his horse closer to Scott. 'We'll give you a day to think about it, Mr Scott. We'll come back tomorrow at about the same time — around sunset.'

'Dyke, any protection I need is right here — at my hip!' As he spoke, Scott slapped his Colt meaningly.

'Don't you bank too much on that, Mr Scott. Don't you bank on it, friend.'

'I've chores to do before full dark,' Scott told them brusquely.

'We're going,' Dyke said. 'And you think over what I explained. You got a nice herd in the river bend, and I bet you wouldn't like to lose beeves like them.'

'I won't lose them.'

'I sure hope not,' Dyke returned, jerking on his reins. He led the three back through the gate and under the wooden Box S sign that was now swaying gently in the breeze.

Scott stood like a figure carved from stone until they reached the road and turned into the east, towards the town of Hartville. He was still standing when a hand touched his arm and he turned with a nervous jerk to Sue.

'Who were they?' she asked hoarsely.

'So you heard?'

'It's the craziest thing I ever listened to. Paying money to to have complete strangers look after your cattle!'

'I pay Pete to do just that,' her husband replied with a wry grin.

'But Pete's a cowhand. Those men are little better than — '

'Yeah, I know, Sue. They're funny critters, right enough. But I've let them know where I stand. They won't come back around here in a hurry.'

'Come in and eat your supper, Luke.' Her voice was laced with concern for him. She led the way towards the door, still looking into the east where a riffle of dust marked the passage of the visitors.

★ ★ ★

The meal was a quiet affair, with Scott chewing thoughtfully and at the same time trying to conceal his worry.

Sue's gaze clung to his face. She made no attempt to shield her own

11

worry. 'When do you expect Reb to get here?' she asked presently.

Scott shrugged, a meagre smile bending his mouth. 'Golly, I'd almost forgotten about Reb. Well, I can't answer that one, honey. Reb was always fiddle-footed. A drifter for sure. Just like a loony tumbleweed skittering in the wind.'

'But you'd like him to come, Luke. I know that you would,'

'No denying that. If the spread goes on growing the way it's been doing, I could certainly use him.'

They were almost through their meal when the hired hand came in. Pete Ferris was lean and grizzled, a man of about fifty or so. He had worked with Scott on Dean Talbot's Rowel outfit before Scott had decided that he had enough money saved to break away on his own account. Ferris was a tireless worker, tough as old leather and completely happy on Scott's Box S.

'Seen some strange jiggers back along by the river bend,' he announced in his dry way as he drew up a chair and Sue rose to bring his meal.

'Four?' Scott wanted to know, and when Ferris nodded: 'They paid me a call.' He went on to relate what Jim Dyke had said and the impression he had got.

Ferris uttered a low curse. 'It's a new game to me, Luke. I didn't like the cut of them. I didn't like the way they were looking our stuff over, neither. I hung around until they caught me watching them, then I moved off. One of them had a laugh like a jackass braying for grub.'

'That's Dyke,' Scott informed him weightily. He changed the subject. 'Pete, did you hear anything of a nester running foul of the regulators day before yesterday?'

'Feller called Garner,' Ferris nodded, his shaggy brows knotting. 'They hung him, Luke. They say they intend to clear the range of nesters and small ranchers.'

'Like us?' Scott nudged. He depended

on Ferris for advice and direction on many subjects.

The other inclined his head. His face was grim. 'I know you're worried, Luke.' He looked round to make sure Sue was still out of the room. 'I reckon that's the reason you sent for your brother. I don't mind telling you that the very thought of them white-faced hombres brings me out in a cold sweat.'

'But they only hit at rustlers. Was Garner running off with somebody's beef?'

'They say he was caught butchering a steer that belonged to Rowel. I've been wondering about Dean, Luke. But why the hoemen come out here is beyond me. They know they can't make a living by grubbing in the earth. It just ain't natural to dig the ground up. And the work is most as bad as hoeing cotton.'

'It couldn't be,' Scot said grimly, an old memory stirring. 'You ever chop weedy cotton, Pete? Or pick it until your fingers grew raw with burr pricks?'

'Can't say I did,' Ferris chuckled.

'My father kept Reb and me at if for years,' Scott explained. 'Down in Texas. It's the most soul-destroying work that was ever invented, and that doesn't leave out cowpunching!'

'Well, I'll have to take your word for it, Luke.'

Sue came in with Pete's supper and the rider smacked his lips and jammed his elbows into the table. 'Sue, that sure smells good.'

Scott went out to the porch and sat down with his pipe burning. The sun had gone below the ragged edge of the mountains and shadows were crawling over the land like grey phantoms, devouring contour and line until the scene became a drab, unattractive monochrome. He wondered if Jim Dyke and his three companions would return tomorrow, as Dyke had promised.

★ ★ ★

In the morning he discovered that six head of his cattle were missing from the lush meadow in the bend of the Boulder River. He followed tracks to a spot known as Parson's ford and crossed, taking his time and trying to still the beating of his heart. The beeves might have strayed, but that was hardly likely when they had access to good grass and water without exerting themselves.

Scott lost the tracks on hard ground and spent a fruitless hour searching the boundaries of Dean Talbot's land. He saw plenty of Rowel stuff but it seemed that his own steers had been well and truly spirited away.

When he saw Pete Ferris at the noon meal he confided in the older man. Ferris swore softly. He lifted piercing eyes to his employer.

'You said this Dyke hombre would come back today?'

'At sundown, he said.'

'I'll make a point of being here. And if that jackass doesn't tell us what he's done with our stock, we'll put the regulators on his tail.'

Scott shook his head. 'There's no proof, Pete. To put the rustling brand on a man you must catch him redhanded.'

'Right. Then we'll scare the hell out of this Dyke ourselves.'

'No, Pete,' Scott objected. 'The right thing to do is see the sheriff in Hartville.'

'That layabout! Say, if he can't stop these regulators from committing plain murder, he can't find our beeves.'

There was sense in what he said but Scott refused to fall in with Ferris' reasoning. 'We'll wait until Dyke shows.'

He spent the rest of the day combing the breaks in the south end of his graze, but he went about the task half-heartedly, knowing that Dyke was putting the initial stage of his plan to collect protection money into operation.

He had Sue prepare an early supper,

then he took his rifle out to the fence. Pete was still working a northern section where he had some cows with calves, and he hoped that Ferris wouldn't show until Dyke and his men had been and gone.

Scott was filled with a strong sense of premonition, and try as he did he could not rid himself of the feeling of impending danger. He had smoked his pipe down to a dottle and was pushing it away in his hip pocket when he saw the riders come round the curve in the Hartville road and take the fork that led to the ranch.

He heard Sue calling from the doorway and he harshly bade her to go inside and stay out of sight. He was tense and grim when the four reached the gate and trotted through in careless fashion. Jim Dyke wore a broad smile and his rolled-brim hat was perched on the crown of his head. He clutched a broken straw between his teeth.

His three companions slowed while Dyke moved out front and put his mincing horse before Scott. His smile was laced with mockery.

'Good evening, Mr Scott,' he said pleasantly. 'Been a purty hot day, hasn't it?'

Scott recalled the frustrating hours he had spent in the saddle, searching for his stock. The fingers of his right hand tightened on his Winchester. Dyke's eyes dropped to the rifle and his stubbled cheek puckered in a lopsided grin.

'Maybe we're disturbing you,' he said. 'Maybe you were just going on a hunting trip?'

'Maybe,' Scott gritted. 'Now, listen, Dyke, before you say another word I'm going to advise you fetch back the steers you drove out of the river pasture.'

Dyke whistled in affected surprise and worked the tip of his nose with his fingers. 'You mean you've had a visit from rustlers?'

'I do,' Scott said shortly. 'And I'm giving you a chance to bring my stuff back. If you don't, I'm going to ride down to Hartville and make a complaint to the sheriff.'

'Mr Scott, I sure hope you know what you're saying.'

'Dyke, you can quit the play-acting. I'm on to your game, and I'm telling you that you won't get a dollar out of me. Now, will you bring back my stock?'

Dyke eased himself round in his saddle, spitting the straw from his mouth. He pulled a tobacco sack from a shirt pocket, jerking his head at the house. 'We could talk better inside, maybe?' he suggested.

'I'm through talking.'

Dyke glanced at his companions. The Mexican Juarez was studying the door of the house with a calculating expression in his eyes. Yance Kibben was paring a fingernail with his teeth. The thin Bob Teal was examining Scott closely, sober-faced and watchful. Dyke got a paper out and poured yellow shreds into it. He spun his

cigarette and placed it between his
lips.

'You got a match, Mr Scott?' he said
calmly.

Scott swung his rifle up with a
swiftness that caused the man to spit
out his quirley. 'Get the hell out of
here. If you don't shift pronto I'm
going to blow you to pieces.'

'Put that gun away.' Dyke snapped,
quick fear washing the insolence from
his face.

'When you show me your horse's
tail,' Scott gritted. 'And if I catch you
near my beef I'll shoot you, for sure.'

'You're making a big mistake,
hombre.'

'I'm going to drill you if you don't
ride out pronto.'

For the space of five seconds Dyke
sat on while dark anger worked through
the lines of his jaws and chin; then
with a click of his teeth he turned the
horse about and shouted at the other
three to move off. 'You're going to be
awful sorry you treated me this way,

Mr Scott. I promise you.'

When they had gone on to the road Scott felt his legs tremble and he was conscious of sweat breaking on his forehead. He heard a horse coming in towards the ranch from the north and turned to see Pete Ferris. Ferris reined his mount to a stormy halt.

'Have they been here already?' he wanted to know, stabbing an angry glare after the riders.

'I put my rifle on them, Pete,' Scott said thinly. 'If that yellow-haired buzzard had stayed a minute longer I'd have drilled him square.'

Ferris stepped down and spat a mouthful of dust. 'Did you find out about the steers?'

'I'm sure they stole them. But there's no proof.'

'Let's go after that outfit,' Ferris suggested forcefully.

'No, Pete. We'll just have to keep a good watch on our stuff from this out.'

It was late when Scott turned in

that night. He awoke in the early hours to hear hoofbeats clattering into the front yard. He was buckling his belt about his waist when somebody hailed loudly and then his name was called.

'It's the regulators!' Sue cried in alarm. 'Luke, I just know . . . '

He was making for the door when Pete Ferris joined him. He hauled the door open and stepped into the star-dusted gloom.

'Luke, don't go out,' Sue pleaded.

'Look after her, Pete.'

Six hooded riders were spread across the yard and Scott's breath rasped in his throat. 'What's going on?'

The man nearest him spoke. 'Scott, we've trailed some stuff to your place.'

'What! Hell, you're mistaken. What — '

'Better take him,' one of the hooded man's companions urged.

At that instant Pete Ferris pushed his boss aside and stepped on to the porch. 'You're a damned liar. We've been missing stock ourselves.'

'Get him!'

Ferris' gun spat flame as the men galloped up to the door. They jumped from their horses and Scott tried to get across the yard. He heard a sixshooter bark and Pete Ferris swore raggedly, tumbling to the ground.

Scott ducked and weaved through the darkness, feet pounded after him. The hooded raiders flung themselves on top of the rancher, forcing his face into the trampled earth.

They thonged his wrists in spite of the fight he put up, then dragged him through the dust towards a horse. He was heaved into the saddle while a man held the rearing beast. All the while scream after scream cut through Scott's brain like a hot knife as Sue tried to reach him.

She was still screaming when the men scrambled into their own saddles, one behind the captive. Then they were gone through the gate and on towards the outer night that breathed stark menace for the woman, the clamour of galloping hooves echoing the turmoil in her breast.

A wind sprang up and raced round the yard, causing the wooden Box S symbol above the gate to creak mournfully.

2

Reb Scott came off the Hartville road and brought his bay gelding to a halt beside the Boulder River. He shifted himself in the saddle and rolled a smoke while he surveyed the winding ribbon of shimmering water where it angled away through good grassland and lost itself in the early morning haze. If he had followed aright the directions of the bartender back in town he should be seeing Luke's place any time.

He recalled the bartender's coolness and his odd look when he inquired about the location of the Box S and once more he tried to find a reason for his reactions. Was Luke in some trouble? Was he or Sue ill?

The letter he had received from his brother two months ago had hinted that everything was not as it should be with Luke. There had been mention of rustling and of not having a big enough crew to mind the stock. It was a mystery to Reb how Luke had got going as a rancher in the first place.

He followed the fork in the road until he saw the squat frame of a ranch house and urged the bay to hurry it up a little. When he topped a grassy rise where wildflowers tossed in the fresh breeze and saw a long mound beneath a couple of trees he brought the bay in abruptly and pushed his hat up from his brow. Frowning, he slid from his worn saddle and bent to read the crude wooden marker at the top of the mound. Somebody had etched a short epitaph. It read: 'Luke Scott. Hanged for cattle rustling.'

A mist came up before Reb's eyes and the sudden pain in his breast was like a savage knife thrust. He straightened slowly and his eyes lifted to the huge arms of this graceful cottonwood. A rope had been tied up there and the frayed end where it had been cut dangled this way and that in the breeze. Reb wiped his clammy brow with a hand that trembled and tried to still the mad thumping of his heart.

'It's a lie,' he whispered. 'It just couldn't be true.'

With an oath he hauled the marker out of the soft earth and broke the board across his knee. He flung it from him and then sank to his haunches where he breathed slowly through his teeth like a man in great pain.

After long minutes Reb went to the bay and hoisted himself aboard. His bronzed face was set and grim and his grey eyes were flinty points of light as he rode on towards the house. How had Sue taken this, Sue whom his brother had raved about?

He was going through the gate where the Box S sign creaked when he saw the grey-haired man on a chair before the porch. The man had been watching his approach and as Reb drew closer he brought a rifle up and levelled it.

'Don't come any nearer,' he commanded ringingly.

Reb kept the bay moving towards him and again the man warned him. Then the weapon fell from his hands and clattered at his feet.

'No!' he cried. 'It can't be — ' He tried to get off the chair but fell back and stared wildly as Reb drew up.

'Oh, lord!' A shudder ran through him. 'I thought for a minute you were Luke. I thought I was seeing a ghost . . .'

'I'm Reb Scott. Is this my brother's place?'

'Brother? Boy, you're the living image of Luke. I thought my mind was leaving me.'

'Who are you?' Reb demanded flatly.

'Pete Ferris. I worked for Luke. I — '

'Where is Sue?'

'She ain't here.'

'Where is she?'

'Out having a look at the herd in the north pasture.'

Reb frowned. 'Did the rest of the outfit leave?'

'What outfit? Mister, there ain't any other riders. Luke and me ran the place ourselves.'

'I see.' Reb glanced over the yard. He wanted to know what had happened to Luke, but he dreaded the answer he might get. He would have staked his life on his brother being straight.

'Can I water my horse?'

'Pump and trough over by the stable. Say, are you going to stay here?'

Reb's eyes came back to Pete Ferris. He looked thin and worn, like a man who was recovering from a sickness. He had retrieved his rifle and now sat with it across his knees.

'I don't know,' Reb said. 'Tell me, have you looked at the place where they buried Luke?'

'You know then?' Ferris said gustily. 'Well, that's something I was dreading having to tell you.'

'Have you seen the grave?' Reb pressed.

'I haven't walked more than a few yards for a month, since — since it happened. Sue has never been near it. She can't bring herself to go. Maybe later on.'

Reb's mouth tightened. 'I reckon it comes hard looking at a rustler's grave. Harder maybe when he was your husband.'

'Hey, you got it wrong, mister.' A change came over Pete Ferris' face and his faded eyes became bright and cold. 'Say, you do believe that your brother was a rustler, don't you?'

'I read the marker. Isn't it true?'

'A marker saying that Luke was a rustler?'

'Nobody bothered to remove it.'

'Well, you can bet it'll be moved right now!' Ferris tried mightily to get to his feet. He teetered and would have fallen if Reb had not slid from his horse and caught him.

He forced the man back on to his chair. 'Take it easy. I pulled the marker out and broke it. Now Pete, tell me what happened. I want to know who hanged Luke and why.'

Pete Ferris started talking. Every now and then he broke off and pinched his narrow lips together. He related all that had happened on the night the regulators had turned up and called Luke out of the house. 'I opened up when their leader told them to grab us. I couldn't help it. I just saw red at the idea of them calling Luke a rustler. They got me in the thigh.'

When he was through, Reb took the bay to the trough and let it have a short drink. Then he turned it into a small corral where a half-dozen horses ran. He walked round the outhouses and mentally praised his brother's taste and energy. It had been a lot of work done for nothing, though. But maybe that wasn't quite fair. There was always Sue, and Reb knew that Luke had thought the world of Sue. He wondered what she would look like, how she would take his arrival.

When he returned to Pete Ferris he

said: 'Have you any idea who the regulators are?'

'No, Reb. I just wish I had. When this thigh wound heals properly I'll have a go at hunting them.'

Reb betrayed his surprise. 'You aim to do that?'

'Don't you?'

Reb lifted his hat and ran his fingers through his dark hair. He wiped the sweatband with a dirty handkerchief and pulled the hat on again.

'Maybe I do, Pete. Has a doctor looked at your leg?'

'Yeah, the Hartville medico dug the slug out and said I'd pull through. No thanks to the killers. They left me for dead.'

'Killers?' Reb's brow furrowed.

'It's a name Luke and Sue heard. Luke said there was something wrong when hooded men were going about, stringing up poor nesters who only killed a beef when they were hungry.'

'Whose cows did they find here?'

'Rowel stuff. Oh, they were here all

right. Somebody drove them on to Box S graze.'

'Who?' This was getting a little beyond Reb.

Ferris told him about the four men who had called on Luke, demanding a hundred dollars a month to protect his herd. Reb listened intently, his frown deepening. He brought out his Bull Durham sack and put a smoke together. He puffed thoughtfully, staring across the green land that glistened in the morning sunshine.

'Did they ever come back?'

'Never saw them since.'

'And you believe those four deliberately drove this Rowel stuff in here to frame Luke?'

'That's what I think.'

'Did you get their names?'

'One was called Dyke. Sue could tell you the others, maybe.'

'When do you expect Sue?'

'Shouldn't be long. She's been in the saddle since dawn. She's sure eating her heart out about Luke.'

'Who owns Rowel?' Reb wanted to know next.

'Dean Talbot. Runs a big outfit about ten miles from here. That's the nearest distance to his boundary line. There — there's something else you'd better know about Talbot, mister.'

Reb waited, putting the picture together in his mind. There must be more behind Luke's death than mere spite because he would not fall in with the protection idea put forward by the four strange riders.

'Talbot was mighty sweet on Sue,' Ferris continued. 'You see, me and Luke worked for Talbot for about two years. Sue was a waitress in Hartville. Both Talbot and Luke courted her, and I was sure that the girl would be smart enough to go where there was money and security.'

'But she picked Luke?'

'She sure did. And she never regretted it.'

'Has Talbot ever called here, Pete?'

'Once since Luke died. Sue had no

time for his sympathy, and I guess she told him as much. Anyhow, he never called again.'

At that juncture they heard hoofbeats cutting in from the north and both men turned to see a rider coming towards the ranch at a brisk pace. 'Here's Sue now,' Pete Ferris said.

Watching her ride under the sign and come to a halt before them, Reb marvelled at the way the woman handled her red pony. He met the stare and questioning look with a small smile crinkling his mouth. She saw that he resembled Luke and his appearance must be a bit of a shock to her. She dismounted slowly and came towards him, grave eyes never leaving his face, searching his cool, steady gaze. She wore a man's shirt and levis, and strong riding boots.

'Hello, Sue,' he said, extending his hand.

'You — you're Reb?'

'That's right. I'm sorry about what happened, Sue.' The words sounded hollow and futile in his own ears.

'You've come too late,' she said. 'Luke hoped you would turn up long ago. He wrote you twice, at least . . . '

'Sometimes it takes mail a long time catching up with a drifting rider,' he said. 'I came as soon as I got one of those letters.'

'You've come too late, Reb,' she repeated. She dropped her dark head then and gripped the pony's reins. Reb would have taken the beast from her but she went on across the yard with it.

Reb waited until she went round a corner of the house, then he brought his troubled eyes back to Pete Ferris. Pete was pulling a wry face.

'Don't pay too much attention to her, Reb. She hasn't been thinking straight since Luke got killed.'

'She figures she doesn't need me, anyhow,' Reb told him brusquely. 'I'll see you later, oldtimer.' He started towards the corral.

'Hey, where are you going?'

'I'll head out, Pete. Maybe I'll have a look round before I move on.'

'But you can't leave just like that!'

Reb was at the fence and calling the bay when Sue appeared from the barn, hat dangling from her hand by the strap. 'Are you leaving again, Reb?'

'I guess so.' She was steeling herself to keep calm and he did not want to throw her off balance. He knew how closely he resembled his brother, and his very presence here must pain her. He would be helping her most now by staying out of her sight.

The bay came to the fence and he ducked through and brought it to the gate. She was still watching and he wished he knew the nature of her thoughts.

'Won't you stay for a meal?'

'I had an early meal before coming here. Thanks, Sue, I'll call past some other time.'

'You're not leaving the territory?'

'Not yet.' He shouldered the corral gate open and took the bay through.

A roan mare tried to get out behind it and he shooed it back again with his hat. 'I think I'll hang around for a while.'

'Did — did Pete tell you what happened?'

'Yeah, he told me everything. No, not everything. Do you know the names of the four men who called with Luke?'

'I remember two of them. The one who did all the talking was called Jim Dyke. The other was a Spanish name. Juan . . . No, it was Juarez. His name was Jose Juarez. I can't think of the others.'

'That'll make a start,' Reb said.

'What do you intend to do? Are you going to try and find those four?'

'I'll look around.' he told her. 'I'd like to find out a couple of things — including how Rowel beeves came to be on Luke's land.'

That heightened the colour in her cheeks and she met his gaze with something like defiance. 'I've asked Dean Talbot about that. He said he had no idea why anyone would steal his stock and drive it over here.'

'Does Talbot believe that Luke rustled the beeves?'

'I don't know. Look, Reb, you can't just ride off like this. Come inside and have a meal. We can talk afterwards.'

'I don't want to trouble you, Sue. I figure you have enough on your hands at the minute.

'I can't turn Luke's brother away, just when he arrives.'

'You can if you want to.' He accompanied this with a candid look that clashed with some bright fire in her eyes. There was indecision there, hint of conflict working in the woman's breast.

'I don't want to, Reb,' she said. 'Put your horse back and come into the house.'

She went on to the front of the ranch and Reb stood, fingering the bay's mane, trying to decide on the best thing to do. At least, there was no harm in hearing all that Sue would have to tell him. It would revive memories that would hurt her, but it might help him to get a better idea of what he would be up against when he set out to find the men who had hanged Luke.

Reb meant to find them, no matter how long it took.

Pete Ferris mustered a grin when he got round again. He jerked his head at the open door. 'Sue said to go right in. Don't take it to heart if she seems a bit sharp. That girl has come through a lot.'

Reb grunted something and went on to the door, pulling his hat from his head. The living room was small, cool and shadowy; the furniture home-made and strong, and Reb remembered how handy Luke had always been with hammer and saw. He sat down at a window where he could see Pete Ferris and the faint trail that wound away from the gate to the road he had travelled over.

Sue came in from another room and pulled the door shut behind her. She had an apron about her waist and her long, dark hair was swept back from her shoulders and held with a piece of blue ribbon. Reb could not help but admire the graceful form of this wife of his brother's and he pulled his gaze back to the window after one sweeping glance. If Sue had noticed the appreciation in his look she gave no sign when she asked: 'What would you like to eat?'

'A cup of coffee is all I want now,' he told her. 'I had breakfast before coming on here.'

'You stayed overnight in Hartville?'

'I did. I didn't see much of the town, though. It was dark.'

She went through another door into what Reb guessed was the kitchen and soon he heard coals being raked in a stove and the rattle of a pot lid. In a minute she came out with a pail.

'I need some water.'

'I'll get it.'

He took the bucket and crossed the yard to the pump. Pete Ferris seemed to be dozing. When Reb went into the house again he frowned when he saw Sue on a chair with her elbows resting on the table and her face hidden in her hands. She was sobbing bitterly.

'Sue,' he said quietly. 'I'm sorry if my coming here has upset you. I won't stay. I'll just drop by now and again.'

'No, Reb, no!' She brought a tear-stained face up to him. 'I'm only acting like a baby. I don't want you to go just yet. Here, give me the pail.'

She dabbed at her eyes and took the bucket of water into the kitchen. Reb resumed his seat and brought out the makings, his forehead wrinkled in troubled thought. He guessed the woman was about all in. She was minding the cattle and she was looking after the house as well. Then there was Pete Ferris. If only Pete could fend for himself things would not be so tough for her. An idea came to him and he toyed with it before pushing it away. Of course he could not stay here under this roof with his brother's wife. It would not be fair to Sue. And maybe it would not be fair to himself . . .

He had smoked his cigarette down to the stub when Sue came in with a coffee pot and cups on a tray and placed the tray on the table. She had regained her composure and he marvelled at the strength and courage of this woman who apparently intended running the ranch on her own.

He pulled a chair over and stirred sugar into a cup of black, fragrant coffee. Sue went to the window and looked out and he followed her gaze. 'Pete must have got a nasty hurt,' he said.

'The doctor says he should be able to sit a saddle in another month.' She straightened the curtains and lifted a tendril of hair from her forehead.

'Do you think you can manage until then? You've taken on a mighty big job, you know.'

'I do know,' she agreed. 'It was getting too big for Luke and Pete.

That's mainly why he asked you to come here.'

'So Luke thought I'd stay and help with the running of the ranch? I understood he was worried about rustlers.'

'He told you so, didn't he?'

'Yeah, he did, Sue. Do you know how many head of stock you own altogether?'

'I'm not entirely sure. I — ' She broke off and turned to the window as Pete Ferris shouted. She peered towards the trail leading to the gate. When she faced Reb again she had gone very pale.

He rose. 'What's the matter?'

'There are four riders coming off the road. They're heading this way.'

Reb had reached the window in two quick strides when a rifle boomed close at hand. He hurried outside and found Pete Ferris levering a shell into the breech of his smoking Winchester.

'Hold it, Pete.'

'I got one of them, anyhow,' Ferris

grated and Reb lifted his gaze to the four men on the trail.

Sure enough, one of them was slumped across his horse's neck. The other three were hauling their frightened broncs about. One of them caught the reins of the wounded man's mount and started back the way they had come. The other two followed suit and Reb watched grimly as they headed for the Hartville road. He brought his flinty eyes round to the man in the chair.

'You darned fool,' he snorted. 'They might be lawmen, for all you know. You're sure asking for trouble.'

'Lawmen nothing, Reb. It's Dyke and his three friends. I know all about that yellow-haired coyote.'

'Did you shoot Dyke?'

'Naw, it was one of the others I got.'

Sue had come out and now she stood beside them. A glance at Ferris told her what had happened and she laid a hand on Reb's sleeve. Strangely, it was as though her fingers transmitted some vibrant current and Reb hastily started over the yard to the corral.

'Reb, where are you going?' she called after him.

'I want to talk with those gents,' he replied curtly. 'They would have come right up here if Pete hadn't triggered.'

'I'll nail every sidewinder that puts his nose towards this ranch,' Ferris said vehemently. 'I'm no use for much at the minute, but at least I can act as a watchdog for Sue.'

'But Pete, you can't shoot at everyone who comes here,' she protested. 'It'll bring the law and then we'll be in real trouble.'

'Sue, the law in Hartville ain't worth shucks nohow.'

They watched Reb bring his bay out and begin saddling. He rammed his rifle into the boot and adjusted his gunbelt, then he climbed aboard. 'I'll see you all soon,' he told them and put his horse through the gate.

When he reached the point where the ranch fork joined the road, the four riders had already disappeared. The road was lined for some distance with maples and oaks, and wound this way and that, but when he reached a level stretch where he had a clear vision of the white, dusty ribbon for half a mile there was still no sign of the riders and he reined in.

To the left of the road the trees thickened. True, there were numerous avenues and game trails through the green and russet undergrowth, but he could hardly imagine the three riders taking their wounded companion into the woods. If he was badly hurt the logical thing would be to make for town and hunt up a doctor. But maybe the four had reasons for not wanting to ride openly into Hartville.

Another mile along, the road took him into open country. There was plenty of beef here, grazing on the long grass, but although he searched the terrain on all sides he failed to see sign of the four horsemen. They must have taken to the trees and climbed into the higher timber where it swept up and back into the wild fastness of the mountains.

He could not quite understand why the men had been so easily scared off, and yet he knew from past experience that sometimes one bold move at the right moment had more effect than a lot of talk.

Reb considered turning about and going back to the ranch, but then he decided he might as well ride on to town and have a good look at it in daylight.

It was still early morning when he rode off a timbered shelf and followed the rutted stage route down into the sprawling huddle of buildings that comprised the town of Hartville.

The town had grown without thought of plan or design, and houses and stores of various shapes and dimensions bordered a wide roadway. Numerous side alleys branched off the main drag and these ended up mostly in heaps of junk and rubbish that had evidently accumulated since the town's inception.

Reb put his bay through the morning traffic, squinting at the timber and abode structures. Presently, he saw a sign that read 'Sheriff' and underneath the word, 'Jail.'

'I guess I'll start here.' He brought his horse in at the sagging hitchrail, at the same time aware of a fat man who was watching his every move.

3

He was sitting on a bench at the front of the law office with his hat slanted over his face. Although he pretended not to be interested in the newcomer, Reb knew he was being sized up minutely. He became more keenly aware of the scrutiny as he mounted the duckboards. He fancied that a tension gripped the fat man who moved slightly so that the sun struck squarely on the law badge pinned to his vest.

'Are you the sheriff?' Reb queried mildly.

At that the hat was slowly pushed up and pale eyes that were alive with curiosity and suspicion searched for sign of sarcasm. Reb's features were perfectly sober and the lawman grunted, rubbing his bristled chin with his shirt cuff. He was obese, heavy-jowled and surly. He was thick in the neck as well as in the middle.

'I'm the sheriff,' he acknowledged with a lift of bushy eyebrows. 'Name is Eli Baker. And I guess yours is Scott.'

'That's right.'

'You sure favour your brother,' the other went on. He roused himself from the bench with great effort and lifted his sagging gunbelt up over his fat stomach. 'I suppose you're going to ask me if I know anything about Luke getting strung up?'

'Do you?' Reb asked flatly.

The small mouth hardened into a straight line and the pale eyes flickered over Reb from the feet up. 'I don't,' he said. 'All I have for it is that your brother was caught with Rowel steers.'

'But you know they were planted there, just so Luke would be blamed for stealing them?'

The sheriff gave a dry laugh and shook his head slowly. His stare was scornful. 'Now, I sure don't know that, boy. Like I said, he was caught with beeves that didn't belong to him. I don't know how they got there, and I don't know why anyone should try to do him down. Of course, I don't hold with these illegal hangings, but I can't do much to stop them, neither.'

'I guess you've tried?' Reb's voice was smooth but his eyes were chill and hard as he tried to control the sharp edge of temper that chafed him.

'If I knew who the hooded men were I'd soon put an end to their game,' was the measured response. 'But I'd like to warn you. If these gents have put the rustling brand on your brother's spread, you'd better look out.'

'You mean they might plant more stuff so they can get rid of me too?'

'I'm just telling you to be on the look-out, Scott. By the way, are you staying at the ranch?'

Reb knew by the light in his eyes that he was thinking of Sue. He hesitated for the space of a second before he said firmly: 'I am. I intend to stay around until I find out who drove that Rowel stuff on to Luke's graze.'

'I wish you luck, Scott. You'll need it, boy.'

It was the end of the interview and Reb turned away, convinced that Pete Ferris had been right when he said that the law in Hartville wasn't worth shucks. Eli Baker was fat and lazy, and unless Reb was greatly mistaken he would lean heavily on the side of the regulators. Likely he figured they were making his own chores easier by instilling fear in the hearts of potential wrongdoers. It was a queer set-up all right, and Reb realized that it was going to be no simple task to catch the killers of his brother.

A short distance from the sheriff's office there was a saloon called the Cowman's Bar and Reb took his horse along and tied it at the hitchrack. The best place to feel the pulse of a town was in a saloon and Reb went through the red-painted doors, hoping to pick up some useful information.

The saloon was doing a good trade, considering the time of day, and Reb went over to the counter where men stood talking and drinking, and ordered a beer. The bartender stared at him and then went to draw his beer. He took the money which Reb slapped on the counter and then glanced at the others ranged on either side.

They were mostly townspeople and cattlemen, and as Reb took a pull of his drink he sensed a lull in the hum of conversation. He frowned, taking a look at the men nearest him. He was greeted on all sides by cold, curious stares that sent a little tingling rippling along his backbone. What was wrong here? Why were they looking at him in this fashion?

He finished his beer and took cigarette makings from his shirt pocket. Instinct told him to get out of here fast. But a stubborn streak made him stand on and roll his smoke. Now that he remembered, he had sensed this same coldness in the clerk at the hotel where he had spent the night before going on to Luke's place. Irritation lifted in him.

He struck a match and puffed his cigarette to life. He knew he should walk calmly through the doors and get out of the town. Luke's being strung up had put some kind of label on anyone connected with Box S, and the striking resemblance between him and his brother was unmistakable. He looked at the bartender again and ordered another drink.

He could not fail to see the questioning glance the bartender slanted at a tall cowman who stood with his elbows placed on the counter, and the slight shake of the head he received in reply. The drink-server coloured but his jaw set in firm lines.

'You just got the last,' he told Reb.

Now the silence and the tension were spreading beyond the counter where Reb stood, and men at nearby tables lifted their heads to cast wondering stares in his direction. The tall cowman seemed to be looking at himself in the back-bar mirror. He was cool and still-faced, and Reb sought to catch the reflection of his eyes. He said to the barkeep: 'You mean the beer is all finished?'

'Yeah, that's it!'

'I'll try a whiskey then,' Reb said slowly. He knew he was getting a broad hint and that they were giving him a chance to clear out, but he made up his mind to see this thing through.

'Whiskey's done, too,' the bartender said, running his tongue over dry lips.

'I think you're a liar,' Reb said quietly. 'I think you've some reason for not wanting to serve me, and I want to know what it is.'

The bartender's eyes darted to the cowman who was now poking his ear with a finger. 'Tell him, Fred,' he said.

Reb swung round to the other. Two men separated them and they eased out from the counter and backed off among the tables, and Reb and the tall man looked at each other.

'I'd rather you'd tell me,' Reb said icily. 'Seeing as how you seem to be paying the barkeep's wages.'

'Sure.' The man smiled lazily. He was wide in the shoulders and muscular in the chest. He was young, and handsome after a fashion. He was dressed in better than average cowhand gear.

'I'll tell you, all right. Rustlers and friends of rustlers are not permitted to drink in this saloon. In this town, for that matter.'

A red haze swam before Reb Scott's eyes and his breath caught harshly in his throat as he said: 'Who are you?'

'You don't know?'

'I don't know.'

'It was my beef they found on your brother's spread.' The smile widened and Reb swallowed with difficulty.

'Then you're Dean Talbot?

'You've said it.'

'Listen, Talbot, you're wrong about

Luke being a rustler. Luke wouldn't have taken a cent that wasn't his own. If he was a thief you wouldn't have kept him working for you for two years. It doesn't make sense.'

'I was as surprised as anybody when I heard what had happened,' Talbot said. 'I don't side with the regulators, but I've heard they make pretty certain of their facts before they act.'

Reb's jaw knotted. 'You really believe that Luke stole your beef?'

Talbot shrugged. 'The regulators had been watching him,' he said.

'Who are the regulators?' Reb countered.

He heard the bartender cough at his back and was conscious of a heightening of the tension that pervaded the bar room. It seemed he was really treading on dangerous ground here.

'Nobody knows that,' Talbot answered slowly. 'And believe me, you don't want to go trying to find out who they are.'

'That's what I intend doing,' Reb

59

replied grimly. 'And nobody will hold me back, Talbot. I'll get to the bottom of this deal if it's the last thing I do, and if you run into any of those killers you can tell them that.'

The insinuation was plain and Reb faced Talbot with burning eyes while a paleness ran through the rancher's cheeks. Talbot forced a small, derisive laugh and made a gesture with his hand.

'Take it easy, Scott,' he warned. 'It strikes me you don't know what you're talking about.'

'Don't worry, mister. I'll find out in good time.'

Reb dropped his dead cigarette at his feet and crossed the floor of the saloon. Chairs were scraped back out of the way and the silence held until he reached the batwings and shouldered outside into the bright heat. He almost walked into the fat figure of the sheriff.

'Scott, I should have warned you,' the lawman said. 'The Cowman's Bar is strictly a cattleman's saloon.'

'You saw me head for it,' Reb said tautly.

'Yeah, but I couldn't reach you in time.'

'You mean you thought they'd take the raw edge off me in there? Anyhow, I'm a cattleman, not that I see how it matters.'

'Well, they gave a nester a rough passage in there one time.'

'I wouldn't doubt it at all. Tell me, does Talbot own this place?'

'He has a big interest in it. He has an interest in quite a few of the business houses in town.'

'Maybe he has an interest in the regulators, too, Sheriff.'

The lawman's eyes widened and his mouth went slack. 'Never let anybody hear you say things like that, Scott. These regulators aren't particular about who they — ' He broke off, knowing he had made a mistake and Reb grinned savagely.

'I understand, Sheriff. They're not particular about who they use for tree decorations. Now I'm getting somewhere, and I'm telling you right now that I'll bust that outfit. Just wait and see if I don't!'

He brushed the lawman aside and went to the rack for the bay. He swung aboard and nudged it on along the road. He had said too much. He had declared his intentions and now they would be on their guard. Maybe the sheriff was in with the masked killers to the hilt.

At a high-fronted store where rifles and revolvers were displayed, he dragged the bay to a halt and went into the place. He bought a box of .45 shells and stowed it in his saddlebags. He stood looking up and down the busy thoroughfare, thinking about the four men whom Pete had scared off with his rifle. Maybe they would return to the ranch when they had attended to the wounded member of their party. Maybe he should get back to Luke's place in case they did turn up.

He was about to mount when he

heard somebody call his name from the sidewalk. He turned to see a skinny oldtimer in shabby clothes beckoning him. Reb frowned and stepped back to the warped planking in front of the store. He had never seen the man before in his life.

'You called me?' he said.

The other had a bony, hungry-looking face. He was about sixty or so, and was dressed in cord trousers and a patched shirt. A battered hat crowned a shock of greying hair that reached to his shoulders. Reb feared he was a crank of some sort.

'The name's Fraser, Mr Scott. Hack Fraser. I heard what you said in the saloon about the regulators.'

'Yeah?' Reb's frown deepened. Fraser must have lined him up as an easy touch. 'So you heard what I said?'

'Maybe I could help you, Mr Scott,' Fraser went on, glancing furtively about him.

'In what way?' Reb asked coolly. He

would have to be cautious here. This man could be hired by the regulators to keep his ear close to the ground.'

'I might be able to tell you what you want to know. It's names you want, ain't it?'

Reb nodded. 'You'd better watch what you're saying. Hack. You could land yourself in a heap of trouble.'

'I can take care of myself, I guess.'

Reb considered the weather-beaten face and the shrewd eyes of the man. He smelt of whiskey and was most likely bothered by a heavy thirst just then. 'All right,' he said. 'I'll be glad to hear anything you can tell me.'

'I hate to bring up the question of money,' Fraser said, his nose twitching in affected embarrassment. 'But it's sure helpful when you're down to your last buck.'

'How much?' Reb asked brusquely, convinced that the man was bluffing and sure that he could not know anything about the men who had hanged Luke.

'Ten dollars would be a powerful help . . . '

Reb whistled. 'You can say that again. But how would I know that you'd tell me the truth?'

'What I'd tell you would prove I'm telling the truth. I don't like these fellars that ride around in the dark, and I'd sure like to see them get a bellyful of their own medicine. Maybe you're the man who can do it. I don't know.' Again Fraser cast anxious looks all about him. 'You want to buy what I can tell you, Mr Scott?' he demanded urgently.

'I'll risk it,' Reb said abruptly. 'Where can we talk?'

'There's an old barn at the north end of the street,' Fraser told him. 'I'll be there right after sunset. But don't forget the dinero. No money, no talk! Be seeing you, I hope, Mr Scott.' He slouched off into the shadows thrown by the store overhangs.

Reb's brow puckered in thought. Had Fraser merely been trying to make a fool out of him, or did he really know something that might help him unmask the regulators? He decided he had nothing to lose by listening to Fraser, and if he thought he was being spun a tale he could soon force him to return the money.

He led the horse along the road to the livery he had used last night. He would spend the rest of the day giving the town the once-over. Later, when he had seen Hack Fraser, he would ride out to Sue and see if everything was all right at the ranch.

At sunset he had a meal in the hotel, then he took his horse from the stable and made his way to the north end of the street. Shadows had thickened and lights had sprung up in the saloons along the wide roadway. Horsemen kept coming and going through the fetlock-deep dust and he wondered if Dean Talbot was still in town. He recalled what Pete Ferris had said about Talbot thinking Sue would have married him. Would the disappointment Talbot had suffered be enough reason for him wanting to put Luke out of the way?

His mind was still buzzing when he reached the last clipboard building that shouldered into the encroaching gloom and saw the sagging frame of the old barn. He had viewed the place earlier in the day so that he would have no trouble finding it. He brought the bay round to the back and left it with reins trailing over its face. He approached the door with hand close to the .45 at his hip. There was just the possibility that Fraser had been told to bait a trap for him, and he meant to be ready for such an eventuality.

In the darkness of the opening he halted and said crisply: 'Are you there, Hack?'

No sound answered him and he took a step inside. A second step brought him closer to a shadowy something that dangled to and fro like a giant pendulum. A sudden icy coldness danced madly along his spine. The

man hanging in the barn was Hack
Fraser.

★ ★ ★

Before Reb had recovered from the
initial shock he heard a step outside
the barn. With a low curse he dragged
his gun loose and had it lifted when a
thick shadow filled the doorway.

'Hey, what goes on here?' came a
querulous demand.

'Stay right where you are!' Reb
barked at him. 'Throw your hands
up.'

He was immediately obeyed and he
stared when he recognised the form of
Sheriff Eli Baker. Still, he held on to
the gun, edgy and trigger-itchy. Baker
backed off slowly.

'Well, it's you, Scott. What the devil
are you doing here with a gun in
your paw?'

'What are you doing here?' Reb flung
back tautly.

'Hey, there's something funny going

on!' Baker erupted. 'Put that gun up, mister, or I'll throw you into a cell quicker'n you can think.'

Reb glanced through the door. There was nobody here but the sheriff. He pushed his gun away and jerked his head. 'Have a look.'

Baker came on into the barn and almost walked into the body that swung gently like some grotesque thing that still clung to a spark of animation. He stepped back with a shocked cry. 'What the hell — '

Reb told him to strike a match. When this was complied with he took a clasp-knife from his trousers pocket and sawed through the strong hemp rope. He grabbed Hack Fraser before the body hit the ground and eased him down. He worked at the cruel knot that had bitten into the skinny throat, fingering feverishly in case there was life in Fraser. The sheriff scraped another match alight that burned for long enough to see the gaping mouth and staring eyes. Then the lawman flung the match aside and turned away, coughing. Reb freed the knot and tore open the patched shirt. He put his ear to the emaciated chest, listening until he was certain there was no sign of life.

He rose then and pushed his hat away from his clammy brow. A long shudder ran through him and he gritted his teeth, telling himself that this was no time for weakness. Eli Baker had gone to the door and he said from there: 'Dead, ain't he?'

'He is,' Reb sighed. 'Tell me, Sheriff, what brought you to this old barn?'

Piercing eyes tried to find his. 'Don't get any funny notions, friend. That's a question you'll have to answer.'

'He said he would meet me here,' Reb told him.

'Hack Fraser meet you here? What for?'

'We were going to have a talk. About the regulators.'

Baker swore. 'Scott, I warned you. I told you to keep away from anything like this. You've no idea about what you're trying to fight.'

'I have, though,' Reb amended stiffly. 'Sneaking coyotes and murdering wolves. Imagine doing this to a harmless old . . . ' His voice trembled away.

'You're to blame,' the lawman retorted furiously. 'Hack never did anything to anybody in his life. He was just a town drunk that wouldn't harm a fly. Now he's dead, just because you got him here to talk to you.'

'No, Sheriff. That's not the whole reason. He was killed because he knew something about these regulators.'

'Scott, how long have you been here?' Baker asked with a new note in his voice.

'Don't get stupid notions. I didn't do it. It would take a couple of men to get him swinging the way he was.'

The lawman expelled a gusty breath. 'All right. You climb on to your horse and get the hell out of this town. It's not going to be a bit healthy for you from now on.'

'We'll have to get Hack out of here,' Reb told him. 'We'll need to get the coroner — '

'You just mind your own damn business,' Baker retorted angrily. 'He's dead, so it don't matter how he died. Nobody can help him now.'

'Sheriff, do you mean you're going to try to hush this up?' Reb demanded incredulously.

'I'm telling you to get out of this town and forget it,' the other barked. 'If you don't, I'll hold you on suspicion of murder.'

'Try it!'

'Don't push me, bub.'

'All right,' Reb said bleakly. He straightened his hat and took a last look at the lifeless form at his feet. 'But you know something, Sheriff: this just makes me all the more determined to break that gang of murderers. They're not justice riders at all; they're not regulators or anything else of the sort. They're just plain killers.'

'Get going,' the lawman said hoarsely.

He stepped back to let Reb go past him. He stood while Reb went to the rear of the barn and swung on to his bay. When he came round Baker was still standing like a fat statue, a weak man who dreaded having to take a stand against the men who had committed this foul deed.

Reb nudged the bay towards the gloom-shrouded buildings that flanked the main street. He rode slowly, peering into the darkness on all sides to see if anybody was watching his movements, and wondering where Hack Fraser's murderers could be hiding.

Light spilled brassily from the windows of the Cowman's Bar and he slowed at the rail, scanning the horses standing there. He considered going into the saloon and telling everybody what he had found. If he told them how Hack Fraser had been left hanging in the old barn it might make them put pressure on the sheriff to try and hunt down the regulators. But he discarded the idea, recalling the reception he had received earlier. They would swallow whatever tale the sheriff told them sooner than believe the brother of a man on whose spread stolen cattle had been found.

Reb put the bay on down the street, trying to figure out who had seen him talk with Hack Fraser. Whoever it had been had watched Fraser through the day and had followed him to the barn at nightfall. They had made him tell the purpose of his visit to the barn. Then they had run a rope over the high beam and put a loop about Hack's neck.

Reb shook himself, wanting to get rid of the picture; yet he could not help but feel a needling of conscience. If he had not made the deal with the man he would be alive right now. And who would the regulators pick on next — the sheriff because he might know some of the men who hid behind the white hoods, or himself because he had declared his intentions of running them to earth?

He was in a depressed frame of mind

when he arrived at the fork in the road and saw a light in the window of Box S. Sue would be wondering where he had been and what he had learned. She might even be worrying in case he had run into trouble. It must be nice to have somebody to worry about you and to care if you got yourself into bother.

He forced his thoughts away from this trend. He would see Pete Ferris, hear all Pete could tell him about the men who worked for Dean Talbot, and about Talbot himself. He could spend the night in the barn and take another ride tomorrow. If only he could have a talk with this fellow Jim Dyke . . .

He rode under the sign above the gate and kneed the bay across the yard. The door of the house opened and Sue appeared, a slim silhouette with the lamplight washing around her. She had a rifle in her hands.

'Is that you, Pete?' she called concernedly.

'It's me,' Reb returned, puzzled. He

wondered why she was looking for Pete Ferris.

'Reb!' I'm so glad you're back. Did you see Pete anywhere? I'm getting so worried . . . '

Reb moved on over to the porch railing and slid from the saddle. Sue came down the steps and stood before him, trying to search his shadowed face. Her eyes were large and fearful.

'Reb, I don't know where he is,' she said. 'What could have happened to Pete?'

4

'I thought Pete was in no condition to fork a bronc,' Reb said. 'Has the old coot lost whatever sense he'd left?'

'He's not fit to be riding anyhow,' the woman replied. 'But he must have managed to get a horse out and saddle up. I can't understand it, Reb.'

'You're saying he took off when you weren't here?'

'I was out watching the cattle as usual,' Sue explained. 'I've managed to bring the stock as close to home as makes it easy enough to keep an eye on them. But you know cattle. They just keep making their way back to their old stamping ground.

'When I got home at dusk Pete had gone. I looked in the corral and found his favourite horse was missing. He'd taken his saddle and gear. What do you imagine has happened to him?'

He knew what she was thinking, and she had good reason to be concerned. If Jim Dyke and his friends had come back to take their revenge, there was no telling what had happened. 'I reckon he just decided to try and take a ride,' Reb said. 'He doesn't like the idea of being useless around the ranch. He'll be all right.'

'You don't think those men came here again?' Sue asked, voicing his thoughts.

'It's hardly likely. But if it'll make you feel better I'll ride around and try to find him.'

'Oh, Reb, would you? I'll go along with you.'

'No. You stay here. Keep that rifle handy, and if anybody comes skulking around, let them have a shot. You can handle a gun?'

Sue nodded. 'But I'd much rather go with you. Maybe Pete has fallen somewhere and can't get home.'

'His horse would have come back,' Reb reasoned.

She touched his arm and stared into his face. 'I'm glad you turned up here. I was at my wits' end. You didn't find those men this morning?'

'No luck.' He went into the bay's saddle again and wheeled the horse about. 'Any particular place where Pete might had headed?'

'He said he would ride to Rowel headquarters and face Dean as soon as he was fit enough. You — you see, he has some old pards there and he thought they might tell him something about the cattle that were driven here.'

'A real good notion,' Reb applauded. 'But maybe not such a sensible one in the circumstances.'

He rode through the gate and swung northwards. The heat of the day still lingered in the draws and hollows, and the breeze that fanned his cheeks had a hint of refreshing coolness. Reb rode at an easy pace, always on the look-out for Pete Ferris or a loose horse that would give him an idea where he might find Pete. He thought it strange that

Ferris should ride off without leaving a message of some kind for Sue.

Reb kept glancing over his back-trail as it was possible that the regulators would have put a man to watching him after the Hack Fraser killing. The darkness thickened and presently stars came out and filled the vault of the heavens with a mystical, silvery radiance. He crossed a gurgling creek and skirted a section of low hills that were mostly covered with timber and brush.

He reckoned he had travelled about ten miles when he saw a faint glow lifting and falling, off on his right. He angled in that direction, suspecting that the glow marked a fire. If it was a campfire then it could not be so far away.

The light disappeared and the ground became rougher, and several times the bay's hooves clicked sharply on rock. Reb slowed, coming into an area of small rocks and boulders where the horse might easily stumble. When he could clearly see the glow of the fire again he slid from his saddle and draped the reins over the bay's face. Then, sixshooter in hand, he moved forward, halting every now and then to listen.

Voices came to him presently and he tensed. Could this be some of Dean Talbot's line riders, spending the night in the open? Or — and here his pulse leaped with eagerness — could it be a meeting of the mysterious riders known as the regulators?

When he made out the dim shadows of men scattered round the fire he eased himself down and raised his head. There appeared to be three or four of them and they were talking in low voices. Off on their left he could discern horses but it was impossible to tell how many. There was no sign of a guard and he concluded that these were Rowel line-riders after all.

Suddenly a sharp, demanding voice lifted above the others and somebody replied with a brusque order and a harsh laugh. Reb strained his eyes until he spotted a man who seemed to be sitting or lying against a boulder some distance from the fire. He wormed closer, moving Indian fashion on knees and elbows, careful not to make a sound that would draw their attention. He hoped the bay would not betray his presence by whickering.

Now Reb was near enough to make out the figures clearly although it was too dark to recognise their faces. There were four of them right enough, three squatting about the glowing coals and one hunched up against a rock. His eye flitted again to the horses and now he could count them. When he counted five he felt a little tremor of apprehension. Where was the fifth man? Was the spare horse simply a pack-animal?

At that instant there was a slight movement behind him and he whirled, gun lifting to fire. But the man had crawled in close without making a sound and he brought something solid crashing down on Reb's forehead, sending him into oblivion.

★ ★ ★

He came to with the stars shining whitely overhead and he had the sensation of the earth heaving beneath him. Then he heard a voice begging him to say something. Somebody was slapping his cheeks and pushing his head from side to side. Reb found himself looking into the wan face of Pete Ferris.

'What happened?' Reb croaked. 'Where — where are they?'

'They've gone,' Ferris supplied tautly. 'I figured you were dead at first. They must have got the wind up when they found you sneaking around. It's what you were doing, Reb?'

Reb nodded, touching his forehead where there was a sizable lump. He winced. 'Was it you I saw lying by that rock?'

'Yeah, it was. They were rustlers,

Reb. I saw them scouting the ranch earlier in the day. I didn't like the looks of them. Anyhow, I managed to get my nag out and follow them in case they were planning a rustle.'

Reb sat up, filling his lungs with air. 'But I figured you were too ill to sit a horse.'

'I made it,' Ferris chuckled. 'If you're able to move you might give me a leg up and we'll make for home.'

Reb would rather have hit the trail after the rustlers but Pete told him they had ridden away long since. 'It would be useless trying to find them in the dark.'

On the way back to Box S, Ferris told his companion how the four wideloopers had lain in wait for him and dragged him from his horse. 'They tied me up and said they would let me go when they were ready to move on. They didn't strike me as killers. They could have killed me — or you. From the way they talked I gathered they were keeping an eye on Talbot's beef.'

'It wasn't the same bunch that was at the ranch then?'

'Dyke and his men? No, these were strangers to me. But oddly enough, they joked about shooting me.'

'That might have saved everybody a heap of trouble!'

'I don't want to scare Sue, Reb.'

'You don't have to. Tell her you just took a ride. Anyhow, this proves one thing, Pete. There are real rustlers on the rampage.'

'You just bet there are, Reb. I know that Luke had his eye on a couple of shady characters. But he would never condemn a man until he knew all the facts.'

'He was like that,' Reb agreed bitterly. 'It's a pity the regulators didn't wait until they were sure that Luke had stolen Talbot's beef before they hung him.'

'Did you find out anything when you trailed Dyke and his gang?'

Reb wondered if he should tell Pete about Hack Fraser getting strung up in the town barn. But maybe there was no point in that just yet. 'I found out one thing for sure. Anybody from Box S is going to go thirsty in Hartville.'

Ferris demanded an explanation but Reb pretended he had been making a joke. Ferris soon had trouble staying in his saddle and had to call a halt frequently to ease his wounded leg out of the stirrup. Reb warned him against aggravating the injury.

When they finally drew up in front of the ranch house they found Sue watching for them. She had pulled on a coat to ward off the chill that was setting in and she hurried over to Pete Ferris. 'Pete, where on earth were you?'

'Just took a ride, ma'am. Guessed I needed some air,' was the laconic response.

Sue helped him dismount and directed her attention to Reb. 'What happened?' she asked with an edge to her tone that warned him he had better tell the truth.

'He was riding around like a darned fool.'

She stamped her foot. 'Reb, please don't lie to me!'

'Sue, you don't have to ride him,' Ferris protested. 'Say, I could sure use a mug of java.'

'You go inside,' Reb told him. I'll take care of the horses.'

He watched Pete hobble on to the porch with Sue's help, then he brought the horses round to strip them. He took his time over this and lingered at the corral when he was through, smoking a cigarette and turning things over in his mind. He heard Sue call him and obediently went into the house where cups and plates were laid out on the table.

In the lamplight she turned to look at him and then he remembered the bruise on his forehead. 'Did you get a hard knock?' she asked in a gentle voice.

'Knock? Heck, I never knew I had a knock. Must have happened when I rode under that low branch.'

'It's the first time I knew a tree could hit with such a wallop,' she said drily and turned away to pour the coffee.

The meal was a strained affair, with all three trying to appear normal and unconcerned. Pete Ferris attempted to make small talk but failed miserably. His leg hurt and he was trying to shield the fact. Sue kept glancing at Reb until he pushed his chair back.

'I guess I'll get some fresh air.'

'Everybody has a sudden desire for fresh air! Now, if you two are treating me like a little girl you're making a big mistake. I want the truth. What happened to make you leave the ranch today, Pete? The truth, mind you!'

'But shucks, Sue, I just told you — '

She stamped her foot again. 'Don't lie, I tell you. Reb, perhaps you'd better tell me.'

Reb's mouth creased at the corners. 'I reckon my head's going to bust if I don't get some air pronto.' He excused himself and ducked out of the room.

Outside, he found a cigar in his pocket and was about to strike a match when he heard something moving out beyond the fence. He flung the cigar from him and snatched for the gun at his hip. He strained his eyes against the gloom, seeking to make out shape or form. Then a shadow moved towards the gate — the dim shadow of a horseman. Reb's heart leaped when he saw a white blotch where the rider's face would be.

'Stay right where you are!' he yelled.

* * *

Sheriff Eli Baker stood at the barn door until the sound of Reb Scott's horse died out on the street, then he sighed raggedly and took a step inside the dark opening. Sweat beaded the lawman's brow and oozed into the palms of his hands. He found a mashed cheroot in his vest pocket and straightened it out before striking a match.

He stood there then, just inside the

barn doorway, his ears keened for sound, trying to figure out what he should do next. From along the street he could hear the muted jangle of a piano in one of the saloons. From a nearby alley a girl laughed huskily; then a man laughed and swore feelingly. A board creaked overhead in the barn and Baker jumped, grabbing for his gun before he realised it was merely the heat dying out of the bleached timbers.

The sheriff forced himself to look at the body of Hack Fraser on the floor. He wondered if Reb Scott had told him the entire truth about the day's happenings. This brother of Luke Scott would not be frightened off so easily. Once Scott made up his mind about a thing he would follow it through to the bitter end unless something drastic happened to stop him. Like somebody killing him . . .

Baker tensed when the clip-clop of hooves sounded at the corner of the street. He stared bleakly while two mounted men came through the shadows and drew in opposite the barn door. He recognised the tall, well-built figure of Dean Talbot and his teeth bit into his soggy cheroot while a flood of speculation engulfed him. He had no time to search for reasons and motives as Talbot neck-reined his mount in close and peered through the thick gloom.

'Is that you, Eli?' Talbot demanded in a flat tone that sent alarm racing through the sheriff.

'Yeah, it's me, Dean. What brings you here?'

'I was to meet a man at the barn,' Talbot said with maddening coolness.

'Who?' the sheriff queried hoarsely.

'Well, I don't know that it matters much if he isn't here,' Talbot responded. He leaned across his saddlehorn and squinted past Eli Baker into the barn. He emitted a low whistle. 'What's that lying there, Eli?'

'You don't know?' the lawman heard himself demanding.

'What's got into you, Sheriff? You're almighty queer. Is somebody sick?'

'Dead.'

'What! Who is it?'

'Who were you supposed to meet here, Dean?'

'Why, old Hack Fraser,' Talbot answered peevishly. 'I ran into him in a saloon earlier. He said he knew I was an honest cattleman and he would like to tell me something that might help to catch these rustlers.'

Eli Baker wished it were light enough to read the Rowel owner's face. Talbot sounded sincere enough and his story was a reasonable one, but why had Hack Fraser asked Reb Scott to meet him here, and why had he asked Talbot along too? Plainly there was something wrong. One of the two men was trying to make a fool out of him, but which one?

Talbot was off his horse now. The other Rowel man whom the sheriff knew as Milt Forbes stood back while they went into the barn and looked at the body. Dean Talbot struck a match and grunted. He wheeled to the sheriff.

'Who shot him?'

'You didn't look close enough, I guess, Dean. If you do that you'll see that he was hung.'

'Hung!' It was Milt Forbes who spoke and he and Talbot faced each other over the body. Talbot's voice cut through the silence.

'Maybe you'd give me a hand to get him down to the doc's place?' the sheriff suggested. 'He keeps a room for this kind of thing.'

'Why not,' Talbot responded gruffly.

'Then I'd like to see you in my office, Dean.'

'Now listen, Sheriff, don't you start getting any fanciful ideas into your head.'

'I'm not,' Eli Baker snorted. 'But I aim to get things straight. You see, it wasn't me who found Hack in the first place . . . '

'You do tell! Who did find him then?'

'We'll talk in my office,' the lawman insisted flatly.

The body of Hack Fraser was hoisted aboard Milt Forbes' horse and they set off down the dark roadway. Doc Martin was on the point of going out for a drink, but when he heard what the sheriff had to say he told them to bring the dead man in. They were laying the frail body out on a scrubbed pine table in a room at the back of the doctor's place when the sheriff spotted something.

'Turn him on to his face,' he ordered brusquely.

Milt Forbes heaved the body over and then they saw the blood on the back of Fraser's ragged coat. Doc Martin frowned, first at where the rope had bitten into Fraser's scrawny throat, and then at the gash between his shoulder blades.

'This man was stabbed to death,' he declared 'I reckon you've got a sticky job on your hands, Eli.'

Later, the sheriff led the way into his small office and scratched a match to light the lamp bracketed on the wall. Behind him, Milt Forbes paced flat-footedly and put his back against the wall opposite the desk. Dean Talbot, grave-featured and moody-eyed, thrust his hat off his brow and sat on the edge of the desk while Baker dragged out his chair and eased his bulk down on it.

'Sheriff,' Talbot said in a measured tone, 'before you say a thing, I want to warn you about something.'

'Is that so, Dean.' Baker searched through a drawer and brought out another crumpled cheroot. A drummer had given him a box of them once, but the box had been utilised for storing documents, with the result that the cigars kept turning up here and there, among batches of old papers and wanted dodgers. He stuck the cheroot between his down-slanted lips and brought a nervous gaze to bear on the rancher.

'What do you want to warn me about, Dean?'

'Fraser was stabbed right enough,' Talbot said. 'But he was left hanging from the barn roof, and that sure looks like the tactics of the regulators.'

'Yeah, Hack was left hanging,' the sheriff conceded. 'But I didn't see what he was hanging from. Another thing,' Baker said quickly before Talbot could interrupt. 'I can't see old Hack stealing anybody's beef.'

'But you don't want to get in bad with the vigilantes, do you, Eli?' Talbot said quietly. 'I know I wouldn't like to be the one who crossed them.'

'They're lawbreakers, whatever else they are,' the sheriff reminded him. 'And if I manage to get my hands on them I'll run them in.' Baker tried to sound completely self-confident, but a prickling of fear was beginning to touch his backbone and he wished for the grit and determination which at one time had made him a man to be respected and feared. Now he was flabby and slow on the draw, and unwilling to challenge the regulators if he were faced with that option.

'Lawbreakers, maybe, Sheriff, but mighty dangerous men to tangle with,' Talbot said in the same quiet but incisive voice.

'Why did you bring us here, anyway, Eli?' Milt Forbes interjected testily. He was a broad-bodied man with a mop of black hair and a craggy jawline. He shadowed Dean Talbot everywhere and there were rumours that Forbes had been a gunman in his younger days.

The sheriff lighted his cigar, angry at the tremor he noticed in his fingers. He stabbed a look at Forbes. 'I want to know if either of you noticed anybody else hanging around Hack Fraser today.'

'We've other things to do than watch what town drunks are getting up to,' Forbes responded acidly.

Talbot intervened. 'It's odd that you

should say that, Eli. I did see Fraser talking with somebody earlier.'

'Who?' The tingling along Baker's spine grew more pronounced.

'Reb Scott.'

The sheriff nodded quickly, puffing a mouthful of cigar smoke. 'All right, Dean. Thanks for the tip. I'll have a talk with Scott. Maybe he can tell me something more.' He heaved himself to his feet.

'You haven't seen Scott lately?' Talbot queried, watching the lawman closely. 'Was it Scott who found Hack Fraser in the barn?'

Baker inclined his head, keeping his gaze steady in spite of the nervousness that worked in him. 'I'll have a talk with him.'

'You do that, Eli. And while you're about it you might tell him to stay way from this town. You don't want another killing on your hands, do you?'

With a warped sneer bending his mouth the Rowel owner straightened his hat and turned to the doorway.

'Let's go, Milt. We've things to do.'

Baker heard them clatter off the planking and listened while their horses moved away from the front of the office. Then he sat down on his chair again and cupped his face in his hands, chewing at his cigar.

'I wonder about that damn Talbot,' he mused fiercely. 'I just wonder what the hell he's up to.'

He scraped his chair back and drew a silver railroad timepiece from his vest pocket. It was still early in the night and maybe a drink of whiskey would help to straighten out his thinking. He hitched his belt up about his bulging waistline and blew down the lamp chimney, then he headed for the street, humming under his breath.

Baker stood on the gritty planking, listening to the sough of a breeze from an alley over the way, feeling the coolness of it momentarily on his face. He puffed at his cheroot, trying to bring it to life. It was chewed up and soggy and it really had gone dead. He was turning along the sidewalk when a horse and rider plunged out of an alley. Baker halted, swearing as the horseman pushed his mount towards the sidewalk. Then, before he rightly knew what was happening, the man yelled something and a gun blazed in front of the sheriff's face.

The lawman cried out and fell backwards, feeling a hot, stinging sensation in his left shoulder. By the time he had scrambled to his knees and dragged his gun loose the rider was pounding away into the darkness and was soon lost in the dense shadows at the end of the street.

For a moment Eli Baker knelt there while a fit of trembling seized him. He heard men coming out of the saloons and someone shouted: 'What's the shooting about?'

Then Baker was upright and feeling the wound in his shoulder. There was a sticky moistness seeping through his shirt but he was sure the wound was merely a superficial one, and that it wouldn't bother him much. A group of men surrounded him, all talking, all asking what he had been shooting at.

'I was just chasing a dog off the street, boys.'

Somebody laughed at that. A man patted his back. 'Eli, we've got nothing to be scared about so long as you're the sheriff of this burg!'

The man was drunk and his remark earned another burst of laughter. There was good-humoured derision in it and Baker turned his back on them, biting his lip against the pain and walking towards the law office.

Inside, the sheriff got the lamp going again, aware of the heavy thumping of his heart. He took a swig from a bottle in a drawer, then stripped off his vest and shirt, wondering whether he should let Doc Martin have a look.

He saw how the bullet had just grazed his shoulder, tearing the flesh but not doing any real damage. He hunted out a piece of lint and contrived a rough bandage. At this juncture he was reluctant to let anyone know he had been shot at.

When Baker had finished tying the bandage there was a new set to his jaw and a hard light in his eyes as he plundered for a cigar. It was a funny thing, but he felt different right now, clear-headed and light-headed.

Sometimes a man needed to be brought pretty close to death to kill the fear that had been building up in him.

'I'll be damned if I don't show them,' Eli grated savagely.

5

Dean Talbot kept his horse going until he cleared the outskirts of Hartville, then he drew in on the fringe of the timbered bench above the town and waited for Milt Forbes. A lot of thoughts ran through the rancher's head as he sat there and none of them was pleasant. Ambitious, avaricious, Talbot's plans were elaborately and cunningly laid. To be sure, he had a large cattle outfit, but he meant to make it the biggest and most powerful in the country.

He owned a couple of the wealthiest business houses in Hartville and he intended to get his hands on many others, including the bank. So far, each step in his plans had succeeded, with only one exception. He had fallen in love with Sue Drake and had been certain that Sue would marry him as soon as he proposed to her. But a two-bit rancher — one of his own ex-employees — had beaten him to it and had married Sue himself.

That had proven a hitch in his plans, but in Talbot's book obstacles were there to test a man and had to be thrust aside with brute force if not by talk and reason. Luke Scott had learnt, too late, that it did not do to stand in his way, and he had been taken care of in such a manner that no possible suspicion could fall on the shoulders of Dean Talbot.

Now Luke's brother, Reb, had turned up to provide him with another challenge, but the Rowel owner was sure he could deal with Reb as he had dealt with Luke. Then, when Sue was his wife and he had scared off the small ranchers and nesters from the range, this whole Boulder River country would be his and he would control the biggest cattle empire in the southwest.

His horse whickered and he gave

it a touch of the bit, but when he detected the rumble of hoofbeats he knew that the beast had heard Milt Forbes' horse coming along the town trail. Talbot waited expectantly while Forbes pulled up beside him and gave vent to a gusty laugh.

'What's the joke?' Talbot demanded, looking down the dark trail where a fine mist was wreathing in ghostly fashion.

'Boss, you should have seen the way he fell back,' Forbes chuckled. 'Like a turkey with its head shot off.'

'You're sure you got him?'

'You just bet!'

'Let's go then,' Talbot said. 'In case some of the citizens of Hartville take it into their heads to avenge the passing of their sheriff.'

They rode through a stand of trees and turned into the northwest. The sky was glowing with stars now and there was just sufficient light to allow them to jog along comfortably. Talbot was turning things over in his mind, trying to figure out the best way to get rid of Reb Scott.

'He's a mean joker all right,' he said.

'He ain't now,' Forbes responded. 'He ain't nothing now but a hunk of lard.'

'I'm talking about this Reb Scott,' Talbot told him. 'We'll have to get rid of him. I want that ranch of Sue's.'

'You mean you want Sue, boss? Well, I wouldn't blame you!'

Forbes was unprepared for Talbot throwing out the back of his hand. The knuckles struck Forbes high up on the cheek and he swore. He reined in abruptly, craggy face hard and reckless in the dim light.

'Mr Talbot, don't you do that again. I'm telling you.'

'Don't you speak that way about Sue,' the rancher admonished. 'Come on, I want to ride to the cabin.'

'The cabin?'

'Yeah, I'm going to pay a little call on Reb Scott.'

'Don't you lose your temper like that again,' Milt Forbes said. 'You know I'm a very useful gent to have around. I just killed two men in the one night for you, and I ain't any better off.'

'You will be,' Talbot told him, trying to keep the rising irritation out of his voice. 'You can't say I'm stingy.'

'No, I can't say that. Are you going to flush out this Scott bird tonight?'

'A little scare. Maybe he'll see sense and ride on out of the territory before . . . ' Talbot let the rest go unsaid.

'I know what you're thinking,' Forbes laughed. 'Just say the word! He's powerful like his brother, ain't he? A woman could hardly tell the difference.'

Talbot's response was a growl and Forbes shrugged, touching his cheekbone with the tips of his fingers and studying the broad shoulders of his boss as Talbot moved out in front.

They swung off the main trail and rode into the woods. Half an hour later they drew up before the cabin in the depths of the forest. Milt Forbes brought a whiskey flask from his pocket and took a short drink. He sighed and flipped the flask into the trees. Talbot was out of his saddle and pushing the door. It creaked as it swung open and the rancher stepped inside. In a minute he had a candle burning in a bottle neck. Forbes walked in behind him and watched Talbot as he turned over a box in a corner and produced some pieces of white material. He flung one of the pieces to Forbes and told him to put it on.

'We'll just throw a scare in him,' he said.

'But ain't it risky going along on our own?' Forbes protested. 'If anybody should see us — '

'Are you turning yellow?' his boss taunted. 'If you are you'd better clear off before the rest of the boys find out.'

Forbes swung on him, his quick movement making the candlelight flicker. 'You're making a big mistake if you think I'm yellow, Mr Talbot. I just pulled two tough jobs for you tonight.'

'Won't I pay you for it?' Talbot flung at him. 'You keep on bragging Milt!'

'You'll pay all right, boss. And don't ride me too hard in case you push me into something you wouldn't like.'

Talbot's breath came harshly. 'You wouldn't squeal on me, Milt, would you?' he said softly. 'You wouldn't do a thing like that, Milt?'

Forbes chuckled, tugging off his hat and donning the flour-sack hood with its slitted eyeholes. He pulled his hat on again and jerked his head at the door. 'Let's go visit Mr Scott.'

They left the cabin, both masked now, and rode away through the trees, two shadowy figures with the hoods showing up like white blotches of pale light. They rode silently, alert and keen-eyed, and an hour later they reached the Boulder River and began dipping south.

Milt Forbes was still in front when

they reached the ford and he rode his horse down to the water's edge. That was the moment when Dean Talbot made up his mind about Milt Forbes.

He lifted his Colt revolver out of its sheath and slowly raised it until the muzzle was on a level with Forbes' shoulders. Milt was turning to look at him when he squeezed the trigger and the blocky man seemed to lunge up in his stirrups before slumping over the saddle horn. His mount squealed and went splashing through the cold flow. Talbot let it go. He watched until the horse had gone from his sight, then he pulled off his flour-sack mask and stuffed it into a saddlebag. He pointed his own horse away from the river again towards the north, in the direction of his Rowel headquarters.

★ ★ ★

Reb Scott watched closely as the horse with its white-faced rider kept coming on towards the gate. Behind him in the house he could hear Sue asking what was wrong, then Pete Ferris shuffled out and propped himself against the door post, sixshooter grasped in his hand. When Ferris saw the horseman he uttered a cry of fear and anger and brought his gun sweeping up. Reb knocked his arm aside and ordered him not to fire.

'There's something funny about this,' he muttered. 'That rider is hurt.'

Reb stepped down from the porch and Ferris yelled at him to come back, warning him that this was a trick to get him into the open. Sue was in the doorway now too and she added her pleading to Pete's stern warning. Reb came up short then and raised the gun he held in readiness. He called for the horseman to halt but the horse came on into the yard and then stopped and bent its neck, searching for grass. Its rider appeared to fold in two. His hat fell off to reveal the white hood over his head and then, while Sue screamed, he slid limply to the earth and lay still.

For a long minute the three of them stood there, silent and tense. Reb's gun never left the man but his eyes were darting here and there, combing the shadows for sign of other riders. When finally he decided that this man had come here on his own he started to walk slowly towards him. Ferris called another warning but Reb waved him to silence. When he reached the limp figure he held his gun aimed at the white-hooded head.

'There's no use playing possum. If you don't get up I'll shoot you.'

The man's horse had lost interest in the confines of the yard and wandered back through the gate. Reb's eyes were growing more accustomed to the gloom, and they narrowed when they saw the stain that had soaked into the edge of the white hood. He rammed his gun into its holster and bent to have a closer look. The man was dead all right. He had been shot in the back. He had clung tenaciously to whatever spark of life had willed him to stay on his horse until it stopped, then he had let go. Reb wished he had been able to hold on for just a little longer.

He told Sue to go into the house, but she refused to move from the door and Pete Ferris stood like a lean sentinel, covering Reb in case some other riders showed.

'Who is it, Reb?' he called.

'Don't know. Somebody bored him.'

Reb had pulled the flour-sacking from the man's head and he found himself looking into a strange face with horrible grinning mouth and wide, staring eyes. He had never seen this man before, to his knowledge.

'Come and have a look, Pete. I don't think there's anybody else.'

It took Ferris some minutes to get across the yard. Sue followed on his heels, ready to steady him if he faltered, and Reb allowed her to come within a couple of yards of the dead regulator before he said gently: 'No closer, ma'am.'

Reluctantly she turned and went back

to the house. She stood at the porch railing, watching them while memory stirred the bitterness her husband's death had instilled in her. Sue would have no qualms over looking at the dead regulator. She was glad he was dead and she did not care much how he had met his fate. She hoped the day would come when all the cowardly riders who hid behind those white masks were either killed or banished from the range. On the heels of these thoughts she wondered if Luke's brother was the man who would accomplish this task.

Pete Ferris took one look at the face of the dead man and whistled softly.

'You know him, Pete, don't you?'

'Sure, I know him. This is Milt Forbes, one of Dean Talbot's men.'

'Talbot!' Reb's lips pursed while he recalled the tall, handsome man in the bar room of the saloon in town. 'Pete, you don't suppose that Talbot himself is one of — '

'I wouldn't be surprised,' Ferris

returned tautly, divining the notion in Reb's mind. 'What will we do with him?'

Reb rubbed his chin. His gaze lifted to where Forbes' mount was wandering away from the yard. 'I'd better take that bronc in,' he said and went out to catch the horse.

When he came back leading the nervous beast, Pete Ferris was making a search of Forbes' pockets. 'Look out for messages of any kind,' he told Pete. 'Anything that may give us a lead on who Milt's friends were.'

Reb had to take the fractious horse to the corral. He tied the animal to the fence while he swung the saddle clear of its back. Then he sent it through the gate with a slap on the flank. The beast drew up its hooves and squealed in defiance. It ran to the nearest horse and nipped it, causing the other stock to mill and prance though the shadows.

Reb went back to Ferris. He had decided to leave the body of Milt

Forbes in the barn until morning, when he would ride into town and bring the sheriff out. Eli Baker would not like this latest development in the pattern of things but he would have to cope with it all the same.

'You didn't find anything else to help us, Pete?'

'No. You know, Reb, I figure there's more behind this than meets the eye.'

'I can't make anything out of it, oldtimer,' Reb confessed. 'What's your idea?'

'I figure Milt there has done something to bring his pards buzzing around his ears. He has stepped out of line, and this is the way they paid him for it.'

'You don't think Milt was riding here to warn us of something and was shot down before he could make it?'

'I don't know, Reb. Milt Forbes was never a gent to do much good to his fellow man. But I guess it'll do no harm to be ready just in case some more of the hooded scum follow him here.'

'If I left Box S and didn't come back they would hardly trouble you or Sue,' Reb suggested slowly.

'Are you planning to run out on us?'

Reb studied the drawn features for several seconds before shaking his head. 'I'm still not sure about Sue wanting me around.'

'Then go and ask her,' Ferris told him. 'Or do you figure that because you and Luke were so much alike she might fall in love with you?'

'Pete, that's a hell of a thing to say,' Reb retorted.

'That's up to you, mister. Maybe it ain't. I don't know. I just have a habit of saying what's on my mind. Anyhow, can't you ask Sue if she wants you to stay here?'

'Until I find out who killed Luke,' Reb qualified.

'That's entirely up to you.' Ferris straightened painfully. 'Look, Reb, I'll just have to get inside. This leg is giving me as much trouble as a rattler bite.'

Reb had to help him across the yard and Sue took over at the door. Then Reb went back and dragged the body of Milt Forbes into the barn and covered it with an old tarp. He was sweating when he had finished and he lingered in the shadows while he smoked a cigarette and tried to find out the real reason for Milt Forbes turning up at Box S with a bullet in his back. He tried to imagine how Dean Talbot would react when he heard the news, and in the wake of that thought came another one, a disturbing idea that sent his pulse to beating faster. Did Talbot already know that his rider Forbes was dead?

Reb flung his cigarette away and took his bay from the corral. Milt Forbes' horse dashed over and Reb slapped its snout with a lariat end. He saddled the bay and went out from the house in a narrow circle that grew increasingly wider. It was an hour before he was satisfied that nobody was hanging about and then he returned to the ranch and put the bay into the corral again.

★ ★ ★

Sue and Pete Ferris were in the living room when he went inside, and Ferris looked as though he had been doing some hard thinking.

'Reb, did you look at the brand on Milt's horse?' he asked.

'Rowel,' Reb replied. 'It was almost the first thing I did.'

'Well, you're a slick jasper all right. I just got around to thinking of it.'

Sue wanted to know where Reb had been for so long and he told her he had taken a ride to make sure that nobody was lurking about the ranch. He sat down on a chair and dropped his hat to the floor beside him. Always, when in the company of Sue, he tried to avoid having to look directly at

119

her, but now she stood waiting until he lifted his eyes.

'Reb,' she said, 'there's something I want to ask you.'

'Shoot,' he urged with a thin smile.

'Will you stay on here at the ranch?'

'Of course he will!' Pete Ferris cut in.

'Wait, Pete,' Sue admonished. 'I want Reb to speak for himself. I want to know if he would be willing to work for me until I can get things straightened out, and you are well enough to ride again.' She brought her cool gaze back to Reb. It was grave and candid and it caused a tingle to run along his nerves.

'Sue, I'll certainly stay on if you think you need me.'

'I do need you, Reb. I need someone to help me mind the cattle. I have about a hundred four-year-olds ready for market, but I'd have to hire strange riders to make the drive to railhead.'

'I'll make the drive for you.'

'Thank you,' she said simply. 'We

can wait a couple of weeks and by that time Pete might be fit enough to go with you. And, Reb, there's something else I didn't tell you.'

Reb was immediately concerned. Some of the strain of running this ranch was beginning to show on Sue. Her cheeks were pale and she looked on the point of exhaustion. 'Tell me,' he urged.

'I'm sure I'm losing stock to rustlers.'

Reb's eyes clashed with Pete Ferris' angry glare and each man knew the other was thinking of the four riders Pete had trailed and fallen foul of. Involuntarily, Reb's fingers went to his forehead where the rustler's gun had thudded and fury rose thick and hot in him.

'That's why Pete rode off today,' he told Sue. 'We were going to keep it from you, but as you have been playing the same game, we might as well compare notes.'

'Reb, was it the men who came here the day that — ' When she broke off

Pete Ferris shook his head.

'These were strangers, Sue. They caught on that I was trailing them and they held me up at gun point. Then Reb happened along and one of them crawled up on him. That's how he got the lump on the head.'

'Reb, why didn't you tell me! If you are going to work for me, help me, you must be frank with me in all matters. You do understand that?'

Reb stabbed Pete a quick look and coloured when he saw the older man grinning broadly. He gritted his teeth. 'I do understand, Sue. From this out you're the boss.'

'Good. Now we're getting somewhere. Pete, have you any space in your room where — '

'I'll sleep outside, if you don't mind,' Reb interrupted.

'There's no need for that, Reb,' Ferris said promptly. 'You can bunk in with me.'

Still Reb hesitated. Tongues would wag when people heard that Reb Scott was living at Box S, and sleeping under the same roof as Sue. They might even get the notion that they were sleeping . . . He rose to his feet and shook his head. 'No Sue, I'd rather stay outside where I can move fast if anything happens.'

'You're worried about what folks might think?' Sue challenged. 'Isn't that it?'

'Of course not,' he lied. 'It's just that — '

'Then you'll sleep in Pete's room,' she said with a note of finality. 'Remember, that you just said you acknowledged me as boss of this outfit. Are you going to back out of that?'

He could not be sure, but he fancied there were subtle undercurrents here which he was failing to interpret. He looked at Pete Ferris again and saw that Pete was laughing silently at his discomfiture. He faced Sue squarely.

'It's just possible that folks might talk,' he said bluntly.

'Let them talk then,' Sue returned.

'Luke never got round to building a bunkhouse. He figured it would be a long time before he could hire a crew.'

'All right, Sue, if you're game to risk it, you've got yourself a new hand.'

'I'll pay you thirty a month and feed you, Reb.'

'It sounds like a square deal,' he agreed with the ghost of a smile at his narrow mouth. 'Right after I see the sheriff in the morning I'll go to work.'

'Good boy,' Pete Ferris chuckled. 'Between us we'll lick whatever Talbot throws at us.'

Reb did not miss the frown this brought to Sue's face. She moved across the room to an inner door. 'Pete will show you where to sleep,' she told him. 'I'm tired and I think I'll turn in now.'

'Good night, Sue,' he said and watched the door long after she had passed through.

Ferris' cough brought him out of

his speculation. 'She's a pretty woman, Reb, ain't she?'

'She's a pretty woman,' Reb admitted. 'And I don't need to be reminded of the fact every other minute. Come on and show me where I can get some shut-eye.'

★ ★ ★

Reb was up long before dawn and when he entered the kitchen it was empty and he concluded that Sue was still asleep. He went out to the chill greyness and brought fuel in from the woodshed. The fire was roaring in the stove and the coffee pot was atop it when Pete Ferris came in.

'You're getting the use of your leg back all right, oldtimer, huh?'

'Keeps improving,' Ferris grunted. 'Another couple of weeks will make all the difference. Is Sue not up yet?'

'Let her sleep,' Reb advised. 'The poor woman can do with a rest for a change.'

'You bet, Reb. I'm sure glad you decided to stay on.'

'Luke laid the foundations of a good spread, Pete. There's plenty of prime summer graze close to the ranch, but I'd like to find a sheltered place for the winter.'

'I'll show you where Luke intended wintering,' Pete told him. 'Just as soon as you've the time to spare.'

Breakfast over, Pete wanted to ride into Hartville with Reb, but Reb would not hear of this. He caught his bay and saddled up, then he left the yard. The air was cool and bracing and the sky was brightening in the east when he hit the Hartville road and sent the bay along at a brisk pace. He wanted to reach town early and get back to the ranch to help Sue with whatever chores she had lined up.

He knew it would take a few days to get into the swing of things but he thought he would like working at Box S as long as his and Sue's ideas did not clash too hard.

It was still early when he entered the main drag of Hartville and few people were abroad. A storekeeper, busy with broom before his shop, lifted his head as Reb went past and nodded coolly to Reb's greeting. When he reached the sheriff's office he found the door closed and he pushed his hat back, scratching his head in irritation. He went along the street to the storekeeper who made a show of industry when he drew close.

'Where does Sheriff Baker live?'

'He nearly finished living last night,' the thin-faced man answered shortly.

Reb felt a leap of apprehension. 'What happened?'

Close-set eyes regarded the newcomer suspiciously. 'You really don't know?'

'Would I be asking if I did, man?'

The storekeeper glanced about him furtively before continuing. He coughed to clear his throat. 'Seems somebody sent a horse at the sheriff and took a shot at him, then rode out of town. Eli thought nobody saw it happen and he tried to laugh it off. But Bill Leeper saw it and he says he doesn't know how the sheriff escaped. Bill says he was watching through his window over the mercantile yonder. But when he reached the street Eli was up and there was a crowd round him. Sheriff said he'd been shooting at a dog.'

'Where does he live?' Reb pressed.

'Back of his office. He has a poky room there.' The storekeeper was thawing out a little. 'You're Luke Scott's brother, ain't you?'

Reb nodded, his thoughts on other things. He said thanks and so-long and headed off to find the sheriff.

6

Reb tied the bay's reins at the front of Eli Baker's office and thumped on the door. He waited a couple of minutes, and was about to thump again when he heard a bolt being drawn and the sheriff put his fat face round the edge of the door.

'It's you, Scott . . . What d'you want?'

'I want to report something, Eli.'

'I'll be open for business after nine,' Baker snorted peevishly. He tried to slam the door but Reb had managed to stick the toe of his boot into the opening.

'This could be important, Eli.'

'Hell, quit this Eli stuff! I know your damned ilk. Troublemakers!'

'There's a dead man out at Box S,' Reb said crisply. 'Before you shut me out you might as well know what his name is.'

'Who?' the other queried hoarsely.

'Milt Forbes. Talbot's man.'

The fat face fell into slack lines of surprise and the loose mouth moved a couple of times. He jerked his head. 'Come in.'

Inside the office there was a strong odour of coffee and fried food. A cracked earthenware cup stood on the desk beside a half-finished plate of eggs and ham. The sheriff was dressed in levis and shirt. His feet were bare as he padded over the floor and waved Reb to a chair.

'Want a mug of coffee?'

Reb shook his head. 'Don't let me keep you from your breakfast.' He noticed a stiffness about the man's left arm and remembered what the storekeeper had said. 'Did you hurt your arm?'

Baker waved that aside as irrelevant. He sat down and lifted his socks from the floor where they had been lying beside his boots. 'What about Milt Forbes being dead? Did you shoot him?'

Reb began to spin up a cigarette. He told the sheriff how Forbes had turned up at Box S last night. 'At first we didn't know who he was, because he was wearing a flour-sack mask over his head like a hood.'

'What!' Baker stared as if Reb had lost his senses. 'But Milt was a cowhand. He worked for Dean Talbot . . . '

'It didn't prevent him from wearing a white mask,' Reb reminded grimly. 'The sooner you take him off our hands the better we'll like it.'

'You could have packed him in here,' Baker pointed out.

'I could. But I'm not paid for carting dead regulators around. Besides, think of the scare I might have thrown into the peace-loving citizens of Hartville.'

Eli Baker fumed. He made an angry gesture with his hand. 'I'll ride out to Box S shortly. But I'm warning you, mister, I'm not taking your word at face value.'

Reb's smile was a twisted sneer. 'At least we've come to a definite

131

understanding, Sheriff, and we've one thing in common: neither of us is taking the other at face value.'

Reb left the lawman gritting his teeth and muttering under his breath. He slammed the office door at his heels and went to the bay. When he rode past the storekeeper again he was greeted with a cold stare of curiosity and he grinned in friendly fashion and flipped his cigarette stub at the merchant's feet.

* * *

Eli Baker arrived at Box S shortly after Reb returned from town. The sheriff rode on a buggy handled by a lean, saturnine man with a deputy's badge pinned to his vest. Reb watched the rig trundle into the yard and went out to meet the pair. The sheriff sat on for a minute, chewing at his underlip while he looked around him.

'You wouldn't be playing a big joke, Scott?'

'This is no joke, Eli.'

Baker frowned his annoyance and looked at the front of the house. He climbed down, speaking to the deputy. 'Stay where you are until I shout, Frank.'

In the barn he stared glumly at the body of Milt Forbes. His frown deepened as he thought about something and he scratched his neck. 'He was dead when he got here?'

'Just about. He seemed to be trying to stay alive until he reached someone. Maybe he wanted to tell who had shot him before he cashed his chips.'

'Yeah, maybe.' Eli Baker was thinking of Dean Talbot and Milt Forbes together in town last night.

Reb had dropped the flour-sack mask beside the sheriff and Baker lifted it and examined it minutely. He poked a blunt finger through the eyeholes and then tossed the article to the ground with a gesture of disgust.

'You'd better take that along as evidence,' Reb told him.

'I don't need to be told how to do my job, mister,' was the testy response.

'Look, Sheriff,' Reb said sharply, 'you're going to have to face up to this regulator business sooner or later. Maybe if you do it sooner it might be better for your own health and peace of mind.'

Baker swung on the tall man, brows drawn and nostrils flared. 'Just what are you driving at, Scott?'

Reb allowed a faint smile to pucker his mouth. 'I heard about somebody taking a shot at you.'

'You heard — ' colour blotched the lawman's face. 'Some of the old hens in town, eh?' He yelled for his deputy to fetch the buggy.

With Reb's help they lifted Milt Forbes into the flat-bottomed vehicle. Baker draped a couple of sacks over him. Reb got Forbes' horse from the corral and tied it behind. Then the sheriff climbed on to the seat and put a wooden stare on Reb.

'I'm not through with you. I'll need to ask a heap more questions.'

'Anytime,' Reb answered coolly. 'And don't forget the evidence.' He dropped the flour-sack mask into the buggy.

Eli Baker snorted and ordered Frank to get going. The deputy brought the buggy round in a tight circle and headed back through the gate and off into the clear sunlight. Reb was looking towards the north when Pete Ferris shouted from the door of the house.

'Did he look surprised, Reb?'

'Hard to say, Pete. You wouldn't know what Eli is thinking.'

'I never fancied him,' Ferris declared. 'He's too darned lazy to make a good lawman.'

Reb started for the corral to get his horse. 'I'm going after Sue,' he told Pete. Sue was out rounding up the four-year-olds she wanted driven to railhead, and Reb knew it would be no easy task for the woman.

He had the bay saddled and was taking it to the gate when a couple of horsemen came over a rise in the northwest and rode at a jog-trot towards the ranch. Pete Ferris saw them as well and limped down into the yard.

'More visitors! This ranch is sure getting popular.'

Reb stood, rubbing the bay's poll and watching the newcomers with eyes squinting against the sun-glare. When the pair were close enough to be recognised clearly, Pete Ferris cried sharply: 'It's Dean Talbot, Reb! And Tim Stanton.'

Reb experienced a queer little tremor at the base of his neck and he pushed the bay gently to one side and brought his holster to hand for easy reach. The clip-clop of the approaching horses grew louder until Talbot and Stanton reached the ranch yard gate. There they paused briefly before coming on into the yard and drawing up to face Reb and Pete.

This morning Talbot wore a checkered

shirt and calfskin vest. A red neckerchief was knotted at his muscular throat and the sun caught his highly polished boots and gleaming spurs. Tim Stanton was a squat man in battered hat and well-worn outfit, and Reb noted the two guns thonged at his thighs. He was past middle age and greying, with sun-darkened face and quick, sharp gaze.

Talbot's glance went beyond Reb to Pete Ferris. He inclined his head briefly to Pete. 'How's the leg?'

'Coming along,' Pete replied shortly.

'Good. And how's Box S progressing?' This time Talbot directed his question at Reb Scott and Reb's mouth tightened.

'You ride all the way over here just to find out?' he queried.

'You got a civil question, mister,' Tim Stanton said in a dull, grating voice.

Reb's first impulse was to laugh at the man's cool nerve but then he met the burning arrogance in Stanton's small eyes and anger kindled in him afresh as he recalled how Talbot had treated him in the town saloon. He said tautly: 'Box S is doing fine. Anything else you want to know?'

'Sure!' It was Talbot speaking again, his manner easy and confident. 'I'd like to know if you've seen one of my men riding past. He's been missing since last night and he was seen heading in this direction.'

'You're a bit late,' Reb told him. 'Your man is on his way to town with the sheriff.'

'What!' Sheer surprise washed the smugness out of Talbot's face and his lower jaw dropped.

Reb made a mental note. Talbot did know that his rider, Milt Forbes, had been shot. He glanced at Pete Ferris who was watching him anxiously. 'Do you think they might catch up with the sheriff if they rode hard enough, Pete?'

Ferris coughed and nodded vigorously. 'Sure, Reb. They could overtake the sheriff before he reaches town.'

Talbot's expression was one of

confusion now, and Reb was sure that his hunch about this man was right. Dean Talbot was somehow involved in the death of Milt Forbes. But to what extent? And did Talbot know that Forbes had been a member of the regulators? He decided to toss another stone into the already agitated pool.

'Your man is dead,' he said. 'He died here at Box S.'

Now Talbot was positively worried. He looked at Tim Stanton but Stanton was watching Reb with calculating eyes. 'You mean Milt Forbes is dead?' Talbot said huskily. 'How — how did it happen?'

The rancher was getting mixed up in his acting and Reb had a strong feeling of repugnance. 'I can't tell you anything about it,' he said.

Still Dean Talbot hung on, waiting for Reb to tell him more about Milt Forbes. Reb's face grew grey and cold. 'Milt Forbes came here last night,' he said flatly. 'He was almost dead, and he was wearing a white hood . . . '

'I feared that!' Talbot cut in. 'I suspected Milt was in with the regulators, but I wasn't sure. But who shot him? Did he say anything that might — '

'He didn't say much,' Reb answered. 'Just enough to let me know what kind of wolves are on this range.'

Talbot's eyes glistened. There was a line of moisture on his upper lip. 'Did he tell you who shot him?'

Reb met the man's probing stare. He hoped that Pete would not give him away as he lied glibly: 'Yeah, he was able to tell me that much, Talbot.'

The rancher tensed and Reb noticed his right hand sliding along his leg to his gun. 'Tell me who it was.'

Reb shook his head. 'I'm not certain that I caught the name right, and I'm not saying more until I am sure.'

'I see.' Talbot considered him, trying to gauge him, trying to make up his mind about whether he was telling the truth. 'I'd like to hear what the name sounded like.'

Reb shook his head again and Tim

Stanton said brashly. 'Maybe this joker killed Milt himself, boss.'

'No, I don't think he did, Tim. But I'd sure like to know who did shoot poor Milt. You won't change your mind and tell me, Scott?'

'Just let's say I'll tell you when I'm sure of my man,' Reb returned.

'Right!' Talbot's face lost its tenseness and Reb knew that he had made his mind up about something.

The pair wheeled their horses out of the yard and cut on to the trail leading to Hartville. Reb continued to watch them until they passed from sight, then he met Pete Ferris' questioning eyes.

'You know that Milt was dead when we got to him, Reb.'

Reb smiled thinly. 'I got to him first. Remember?'

'And he managed to tell you who shot him?'

'I wanted Talbot to believe that, Pete. You know, I don't like that man at all.'

'You've maybe let yourself in for

more trouble, mister.'

'Maybe. And again, I might have started something that'll bring things to a head.'

Pete had more questions to ask but Reb was through talking. He swung aboard the bay and told Pete to watch the place until he returned. Right now he felt he should be helping Sue round up the stock that was to be driven to railhead.

★ ★ ★

The days slipped by at Box S, work-filled days and uneventful. Gradually Pete Ferris regained the full use of his leg and once more was able to help Sue and Reb. Reb was a hard worker, enthusiastic, and for the time being at least, totally dedicated to the idea of seeing Box S become a prosperous spread. The weeks ran into months and when autumn came round Reb took on a couple of drifting riders to help with the round-up and branding. The steers were separated from the she-stuff and calves, and on Reb's advice Sue sold the steers when the round-up was finished.

'You'd be wise to get rid of them when they're there,' he told her. 'A bad winter might kill some of them off and you have to consider rustlers.'

So it was that Reb and the two hired men drove a small herd to the railhead town of Elmira, leaving Pete and Sue to look after the ranch. Reb found a buyer who offered him fifteen dollars a head and he clinched the deal without question. Back home, he turned over the money to Sue and paid off the two hands.

Now came the problem of finding winter graze for the remaining stock. Pete showed Reb a canyon where Luke had intended wintering the cattle, but the location did not altogether please Reb. He rode the length and breadth of Box S range until he decided on a valley, not as well protected perhaps as the place Luke had chosen, but offering better fodder and giving the cattle more space to roam about.

'You see the high rocks up there,' he told Pete one day, pointing to the north rim of the valley. 'They'll break the worst of the winds that blow and they'll scatter whatever snow flies so that most of it will hit the opposite walls.'

'There might be something in what you say,' Pete conceded.

At Elmira, Reb had heard news of some of the big ranchers buying shorthorn bulls to cross-breed with the traditional longhorn of cattle country. It was said that the cross-bred calf would dress out at two to three hundred pounds heavier at two years than an ordinary longhorn calf. He was telling Pete and Sue this news at supper one night and Ferris wondered if this was the reason for Dean Talbot stringing barbed wire on sections of his graze.

'You think Talbot's going to have a try at the shorthorn stuff, Pete?'

'Well, it ties in, doesn't it? If Dean

was to buy some bulls and turn them loose, there's no telling that the bulls would be able to read a Rowel brand on a cow.'

'I get your point,' Reb agreed. 'Those same bulls might get to mixing with Box S stuff.'

'Sure, and you can bet Talbot wouldn't like that. How much do these bulls cost, Reb?'

'Well, I heard you can pay as much as two hundred and fifty dollars for a single beast.'

'Glory be! No wonder Talbot is putting up fences. But I've no time for these new-fangled ideas. The longhorn dogie is good enough for me any day.'

Sue had been listening intently, and now she rose to clear away the supper dishes. The evenings were growing shorter and a decided nip was coming into the air. 'You two argue all you want, but the plain fact is that we can't afford to experiment at the minute.'

'You're right there,' Pete Ferris

applauded. 'Old Thunder and Lightning will be siring cows long after these shorthorn studs have dried up and quit!'

Sue left them in a hurry on that note and Reb made the excuse of wanting to go and look at the horses.

Later, standing by the corral fence he came back to his main reason for staying at Box S. He was here to find the men who had murdered his brother, and he knew in his heart that he would never leave this part of the country until that had been accomplished.

Many times when he was out riding the high hills or the brushy canyons and gulches he found himself staring into the distance on all sides, wondering what had happened to the man called Dyke and his three friends. He always hoped to make contact with them so that he might run them to earth and get them to answer the questions he was sure only they could answer.

Again, his thoughts would swing to

Dean Talbot and the body of Milt Forbes lying in the yard entrance with a white hood covering his head. Talbot had never called at the ranch since that day, and he wondered what conclusions Sheriff Eli Baker had drawn from the overall picture.

Several times during the fall roundup he had run into Talbot riders. He had made a point of chasing off every maverick that ran with a Rowel cow and he had instructed Pete and the other two hired hands to do likewise. Talbot must not be given any reason for pointing the finger at Box S as a rustler spread, as he had done in the Hartville saloon.

The days grew shorter and the weather became raw and cold. One morning Reb went out as usual to take his horse from the corral and found a blanket of snow stretching from the door of the ranch house. Now range riding became a really tricky game, but it had to be done all the same.

Reb was anxious to see how the herd

would make out in the valley he had selected for wintering and he headed out one snowy morning through the falling flakes and the crisp, crunchy carpet of white underfoot. It took him twice the time it usually did to reach the valley and when he dismounted at the rim to make the descent he was gratified to see a clear stretch of green running right along the base of the north rim. He had been right after all. That side of the valley would never snow up to the extent of depriving the herd of feed.

He was trying to get a cigarette going when his eye caught a puff of smoke some distance away on the valley flats, and he pulled the bay into cover while a stern frown settled on his face. Surely rustlers would not be operating at this time of year when it would be the hardest thing in the world to drive cattle over snowed-up rangeland.

He hobbled the bay in the lee of a tall boulder and started down through the tumbled rocks that studded the slopes. It was tricky going over piled-up drifts and icy stretches, where one slip would precipitate him a hundred feet to the valley floor below, but he was curious to know who was camping here where the Box S herd was bedded.

He still had about fifty feet to travel before he reached the valley level when he heard a wicked crack and a bullet spanged through the rocks, sending snow and rock shards flying. Furious, he flung himself to the shelter of a boulder where he sank into a bank of pure white crispness. He floundered from the snow and hauled out his pistol. He had left his rifle in the saddle boot and now he saw that he had been careless in not bringing it along. He found a firm position behind a rock shoulder and squinted down through the falling flakes. They were thinning out and he could see the smoke of a campfire clearly, but there was no other sign of life.

Reb stood in the cold, trying to figure out who could have fired the shot and why anyone should be camping in the valley. He stood for a long time, frozen to the marrow, watching and waiting for someone to show, but nothing disturbed the wintery scene. At length, cramped and almost frozen through in spite of the heavy coat he wore, he came out from the boulder and searched the valley floor again with keen gaze. The smoke from the fire had died and nothing moved on the vast expanse but an occasional steer.

He put his gun away and continued to descend, alert and ready to fling himself down if the rifle opened up again. Nothing happened however and he reached the flat without mishap. After some searching he found where a fire had been built in the shelter of a cluster of small rocks. A partly snowed-over bean can lay beside the dying ashes and he concluded that he had disturbed somebody who did not want to be discovered, someone on the run from the law likely.

He had a look at the cattle and,

satisfied that all was well, he climbed back to the rim and went into the saddle. The effort had warmed him and he turned towards the ranch, pleased that he could tell Sue and Pete that this valley would indeed turn out to be an ideal place for wintering stock.

★ ★ ★

One day in late spring Reb went on the trail of a dozen steers that had gone missing from a herd that was being gathered for market. He started out, sure that he would soon recover the beeves from some of the grassy canyons that cut through the hills in the northeast, but when a full morning passed and still there was no sign of the strays he began to worry.

True, there had been little news of rustling activities since early autumn, but it was just possible that some widelooping band had returned to the Boulder River country, and Reb decided grimly that he would not go home until he had found the missing stock.

As he proceeded further into the hill country the trail he followed began to climb gradually, wandering through small patches of woodland and bare, rock-strewn gulches, and grey slopes. Far ahead and to his left the ragged peaks of the mountains, still covered in snow, loomed bleak and forbidding.

In a small grassy park he found traces of cattle having been through here recently and he pushed the bay harder, eager to get his hands on whoever had driven off the Box S beef. He was sure now that the stock had not wandered at all, but had been deliberately stolen and pushed into the hills where it would be hidden and eventually sold to some unscrupulous dealer.

Reb was riding round the edge of a towering boulder when the whinny of a horse just in front of him put him on the alert. He came out from under the beetling rock edge with his gun clenched firmly in his fist, and when he saw the two horsemen on the trail in front of him he hauled in abruptly and froze.

For tension-filled seconds they stared at each other. The tall man on the chestnut was Dean Talbot; his companion was the squat Tim Stanton. It was Stanton who relaxed first. He grinned in lopsided fashion and murmured from the side of his mouth: 'Well you never know what you'll ride into!'

Talbot was slower in thawing. The Rowel owner knew that Reb Scott had wintered at Box S with Sue and Pete Ferris. He was not at all sure of the relationship between Sue and this brother of Luke, but he saw nothing wrong in painting the situation in the worst possible colour, and for a second he allowed something of the jealousy and hatred he felt to show on his handsome face.

'You're out of your depth up here,' he observed coolly.

'I'm looking for some steers I lost,' Reb retorted in like fashion, sliding his revolver into its sheath. He could not forget how this man had tried to make a fool of him in the Hartville saloon. He could not forget either how Talbot had shown up on the morning after Milt Forbes had died right on the Box S doorstep. There was something sinister about Talbot and his crew, sinister and dangerous.

He watched how Talbot drew a long breath to his lungs, then the rancher said with deceptive gentleness: 'Are you accusing me, Mr Scott?'

7

Reb regarded Talbot steadily for a few seconds, then his gaze flickered to Stanton. 'I didn't say that,' he replied curtly.

'You've lost steers!' Stanton said with a sneer warping his coarse mouth. 'A good excuse for trespassing on Rowel land!'

'I didn't know where I was,' Reb protested.

'You know now,' Talbot informed him. 'And unless you've business here, I'd advise you to drift, Mr Scott.'

'I'm going to look for my beef,' Reb insisted, hoping to ward off the clash that appeared inevitable.

'You're going no further,' Stanton chipped in coldly.

'Talbot, are you backing that kind of talk?'

'Yeah, I am, Scott. I don't really

believe you've lost stuff.'

'You're calling me a liar?'

'If you like. Maybe you're just spying the land to make a steal.'

Reb came out of his saddle and pushed the bay aside. His face was contorted with cold fury and his hands opened and closed at his sides.

'You've just said something you shouldn't have said, Talbot. If you've the guts to back up your talk, get down and shuck your gunbelt.'

Dean Talbot regarded him cynically while a meagre smile twisted his lips. It was Stanton who dropped from his saddle and stood before Reb. He flipped his hat to the ground, then hooked his thumbs in his gunbelt.

'Will I fill the bill, Mr Scott?'

'It's Talbot I want, friend. I've no fight with you.'

'Teach him a lesson, Tim,' Talbot urged huskily. 'He needs one.'

Stanton unbuckled his gunbelt and flung the gear after his hat. Reb ran his tongue over dry lips and did likewise.

'What about your spurs?'

'Spurs stay on, bub. I'm gonna rooster you, Mr Scott.'

'Let's get it over, then.'

Stanton came in on him, flat-footed, moving ponderously, looking for an opening. Reb turned as the squat man manoeuvred, eyes never leaving his face. Then they were at it, ducking and weaving, pummelling each other. Reb thrust a wicked jab into Stanton's throat and had the satisfaction of seeing a sparkle of fear in the dancing eyes.

Stanton sank his fist into Reb's stomach and was trying to follow up the advantage when Reb slammed a full-blooded blow to the Rowel man's left temple. Stanton stopped in his tracks like a pole-axed steer.

Reb pressed his advantage, launching a savage onslaught that had Dean Talbot sucking breath to his lungs as he watched.

'Get him damn you, Tim! Give him the spurs . . . '

The squat man suddenly fell on to

his back and, as Reb rushed at him, he threw himself up on his shoulders and his spurs swooped on either side of Reb's face. Reb pulled back as one of the wicked rowels grazed his cheek. He knew by the stinging sensation that Stanton had drawn blood.

Before Stanton could get upright, Reb smashed into him with his shoulder, sending him down again. Then he pounced on top of the Rowel hand and commenced beating at his face with his right fist. Reb kept up the punishment until the squat man begged him to quit; even then it was difficult for the meaning of the words to penetrate the murder-lust in Reb Scott's brain.

He scrambled upright finally and stood over the battered cowhand, his chest heaving, his breath a rasping whistle in his throat. Then Reb swung to Dean Talbot. The rancher had his gun clenched in his hand and he spoke through his teeth: 'Get out of here.'

'What's the hurry?' Reb jibed. 'Get down and join the fun.'

'I'm damned if I will,' Talbot cried hoarsely. 'Vamoose!'

Reb gave him a long, contemptuous stare, then he gathered up his belt and buckled it about his waist. He slapped his hat on his knee before donning it. He was reaching for the bay, watching Stanton struggling to his feet, when the squat man panted a curse and charged him. A hideaway knife flashed in the sunshine and the blade whipped along Reb's arm, sending pain spearing to his nerves.

Reb drew and triggered, and the slug from his gun sent the knife spinning from Stanton's fingers. He screeched and Talbot shouted: 'I'll kill you, Scott!'

'Go on and shoot,' Reb challenged. 'See which one of us dies first.'

The Rowel owner lowered his Colt slowly. He looked bleakly from Reb to the gasping Stanton. Reb levered himself to the saddle of the bay and backed it away from the pair, gun at the ready. Then he swerved and drove the beast through the trees.

After a time he examined his arm where Stanton's knife had slashed and was gratified to see that the cut was superficial. Next he touched his cheek where the cowhand's spur had touched him. 'Sure is a nice crew,' he muttered to his horse.

Reb spent another hour in searching for the lost cattle, without success. He halted at a stream and bathed his arm and face, and it was shortly after hitting some scrub country that he saw a track leading off into the woods. Thirty minutes later he topped a bare ridge overlooking a saucer-shaped glade and whistled softly when he noticed the roof of a cabin among the trees.

He began a twisting descent, halting on the rim of the glade and using the shelter of the tree boles to observe the terrain. There was no sign of life and Reb dropped stiffly from the saddle, aware of a dozen bruises on his ribs and chest, tied the bay to a tree and ventured to the front of the cabin. He started to spin up a cigarette but thought better of it and flung the makings from him.

He drew his Colt and opened the door of the cabin. The door gave easily enough on leather hinges and Reb had to blink a few times before his eyes could pierce the musty gloom. There were three rough stools spread round a plank table; an overturned box lay in a far corner. Reb saw a ladder leading to the loft and a search of the small room yielded nothing but an empty whiskey bottle and a couple of cracked cups on a shelf.

Now he drew the burlap sacking away from the window opening and glanced out. The bay was well out of sight and he knew he could depend on the beast to whicker if it scented anything amiss. He climbed the rickety ladder and struck a match to peer round the loft. There was nothing here but a couple of pelts and a cobweb-covered weapon that appeared to be a Sharps buffalo gun.

He descended and headed for the door, satisfied that there was nothing here to concern him. He was about to draw the door open when he heard a faint whicker, and at the same time horses emerged from the trees to enter the glade.

Reb's first sensation was of panic but he throttled it and moved back to the ladder, climbing to the loft and lying down on the ceiling logs. In a couple of minutes the cabin door burst open and booted feet crossed the earthen floor. Then a voice said wearily: 'I don't know about you gents, but I'm sure tuckered.'

'Yance, you're just a lazy hound,' another voice chipped in.

'Oh, yeah? Well, let me tell you, Mr Cole . . . '

'Cut it out,' another voice chipped in brusquely. 'Bob, you go fetch water and rustle some wood for the fire. Juarez, you go help him. Go on — move!'

'Good as done, Dyke,' someone returned.

Then the authoritative voice again: 'Strip the nags, Yance. It'll keep you awake, maybe.'

The cabin door opened and closed. Heavy boots scraped. A man swore feelingly. Reb heard the whicker of blowing horses and the jingle of harness. He cuffed sweat from his brow. His arm smarted and his ribs ached. Who were these men? So far he had counted four, judging by their talk. The names repeated themselves in his mind. Yance, Juarez, Dyke. Dyke . . . Juarez . . . These were the four who had tried to force Luke into paying them protection money!

Reb moved and the log beneath him creaked. Somebody bustled into the cabin and then there was a tense silence. A thin voice broke it.

'I heard something up in the loft.'

Silence again, then the top of the ladder quivered as somebody began climbing. Presently a head and shoulders appeared. Dark eyes tried to see through the gloom. They saw Reb and the mouth opened to yell. Reb leaped out, revolver lifting and swinging down, and Yance Kibben yelled and fell backwards from the ladder.

Reb jumped through the opening after him. He came down with a thump on top of Kibben, went off balance and recovered. His speed had given him the advantage and he swept his sixgun over them. 'Don't move!'

He had a glimpse of one of the men grabbing for his revolver and he triggered wildly. Someone screamed and another of the men made a dive for the intruder. Reb lashed out without mercy, sweeping the figure from his path as he lunged for the door. By some miracle he made it through before guns started banging.

Reb kept racing for the timber fringe, weaving so that the following hail of slugs missed him. He reached the bay and untied the slipknot before swinging into leather. 'Let's go, pard!'

He kept the horse galloping at breakneck speed until the sounds of pursuit receded and eventually faded.

An hour had gone by when he smelled the stench of woodsmoke quite by accident and followed its trailing stain against the sky. Ten minutes later Reb was drawing in before a scene that was not new to him but which, nevertheless, never failed to fill him with apprehension and dark fury. The smouldering pile of timber and clay which he regarded had once been a nester's home.

There was a corral with broken-down poles, and back of the house a plot of freshly-planted garden. Reb circled the scene slowly, coughing when the smoke filled his nostrils. There was no sign of life anywhere, no grazing cattle or horses. There was not even a chicken about the place. Almighty strange. He lifted his head then to look around and his eye came to rest on a scattering of trees on the north side of this small basin. Something moved up there and Reb started towards the area, fingers closing on his Colt.

Finally he saw the sight which he had expected and dreaded. The thing moving gently to and fro was a man, a lifeless man who had been left hanging from a high tree limb.

The bay shied away from the scent of death and Reb slid from his saddle and moved over for closer appraisal. The weathered features were black and the clothing covering the body was dirty and ragged. A shadow wheeled lazily overhead and Reb squinted at the wheeling buzzard. He had his knife out and was about to slash the hemp rope when a rifle exploded viciously and a bullet ploughed into a nearby tree trunk.

Reb spun about, dropping the knife and snatching for his gun. A hard yell told him to forget it and then he was staring at two mounted men who had just cleared the other side of the basin rim. Both had their rifles trained on him. He swore in wonder when he recognised Sheriff Eli Baker form Hartville and the dour-featured deputy, Frank.

'I'm sure surprised at you, mister,' Baker's voice throbbed excitedly.

'Hey, wait a minute . . . I just got here and found him.'

'You don't say, Mr Scott! This is the third gent you've found dead since hitting these parts. Maybe there's more, huh?'

'You're crazy. Take a good look. Do you know him?'

'Nester called Warner. He's lived alone since his wife died.' Baker's eyes switched back to Reb Scott, taking in the state of his clothing and the blood on his shirtsleeve and face. The rifle barrel moved slightly. 'You didn't have a fight with Warner, Scott?'

Reb shook his head. 'Tim Stanton.'

'You're a liar!' the deputy marvelled. 'It's a wonder he didn't kill you.'

'Oh, he tried to. But it didn't work.' Reb laughed shortly. He explained how he had been looking for the stolen stock when he had come face to face with

Stanton and Dean Talbot.

Eli Baker heard the recital through, his fat face registering his amazement. 'You beat Stanton! Ain't that something now.'

'Where's your steers?' the deputy demanded suspiciously.

'Never found them. But I've got a hunch about the thieves.'

'You ain't pointing the finger at Rowel, mister?' Baker probed.

'I can't say any more until I'm sure.'

'Ahuh! Well, let's cut him down, Frank. It's what you were going to do, Scott?'

Reb nodded and stood back while they cut down the body of the nester. He wondered vaguely how the sheriff had come to know about Warner being burned out and hanged. The deputy found a shovel.

'You going to bury him?' Reb queried. 'What about an inquest?'

Eli Baker snorted a laugh. 'Mister, if we held an inquest on every gent that died in this territory there wouldn't be time to do anything else.'

'All the more reason for rooting out the regulators,' Reb retorted. 'You know, I don't believe you want to catch the hellions who — '

'You mind that tongue of yours, mister,' the lawman interrupted savagely. 'I'll catch them in good time.'

'Who owns this land?' Reb asked him.

'It was public domain until Warner homesteaded it. But Dean Talbot always regarded it as his grazing lands.'

'Talbot! And the same Talbot doesn't like nesters coming in here and building fences . . . '

'Talbot's starting to string his own fences,' Baker informed him. 'He's going in for shorthorn breeding.'

'So he needs land? Why don't you come to your senses, Sheriff? They tried to kill you, too, didn't they? Do you reckon they're getting scared of you?'

Baker started to retort but changed his mind. He said meagrely: 'Somebody tried to kill me. I wish I knew who it was.'

'You didn't get anybody for the hanging of Hack Fraser? And you didn't catch the man who murdered Milt Forbes.'

'I didn't, Scott. But Fraser was stabbed before he was hung.'

'True,' Reb agreed. 'I know a gent who figures he's real useful with a knife. But I don't think he stabbed Hack.'

'You have somebody in mind?'

'It doesn't matter.'

'We'll see.' The sheriff put his back to the tall man and looked to where his deputy was digging a hole for the nester's body. As Reb was riding away he called: 'Don't find any more dead men.'

Reb stifled a smile and swung into the southwest. It was close to sunset when he finally rode under the Box S sign and brought the bay to a halt at the corral. Sue hurried from the house.

'Reb, you've been gone for hours. Did you find the steers?'

'Not a hair of them.' He stripped the bay and turned it into the corral where it immediately lay down and rolled over.

Sue laughed. 'I just love that horse of yours, Reb.' She caught his sleeve suddenly and peered into his face. 'Reb, what happened? What's wrong with your face?'

'The bay gave me a toss into a clump of brush.'

'I don't believe you. I thought we were going to be honest with each other . . . '

'Please forget it,' he said gruffly.

'I won't forget it. All you think about is how you can level for Luke's killing. Isn't that right?'

She gasped when he brought piercing eyes to bear on her and clutched her arms. 'No, it isn't. I've got other things on my mind, and — Aw, what's the use? Let's forget it.'

How she came on into the shelter of his arms he would never remember, but then he was holding her tightly and she was brushing her cheek against his face. 'Don't leave me, Reb . . . '

'I won't leave you.'

They both jerked back to the moment when a horse clattered into the yard and Pete Ferris called. 'Well, don't let me break up the party, folks!'

Reb turned to the rider when he dismounted and stood wiping trail dust from his face. 'Pete, you'd better know something. I'm going to marry this woman before she's much older.'

★ ★ ★

The news trickled from Dean Talbot's outfit that he was hiring gunmen to protect the fence he had strung on his range. It seemed that the small ranchers surrounding his holdings kept tearing down the wire as soon as it went up. However, Reb saw the move as another tactic in Talbot's plan to grab the whole of the range.

There were reports, as well, of the success of the cross-breeding, and it seemed that the day was not far distant when the shorthorn would supersede the longhorn in cattle country.

On the Friday of this particular week Sue declared her intention of going into town the following day. Reb frowned at this. He had planned to spend Saturday in having another look for the stolen steers. Reb was pretty certain that Dyke and his riders were responsible for most of the stealing, and he had decided to have another look at the cabin in the woods.

'I'd rather you didn't head for town on your own, Sue. Take Pete along.'

Her eyes blazed challenge at him. 'I want to take you with me, Reb. I'll need the buckboard to bring things back, and Pete has his hands full.'

Later, when Reb and Pete were out on the range, Pete brought up the matter of the stolen beef. 'You're sure they were driven off?'

'I'm sure all right.' Reb told the older man of his encounter with Talbot and Stanton up in the woods and Pete Ferris listened with clouded brow.

'I just know that Talbot's mixed in with the outlaws,' he said. 'With the regulators too, maybe. And Reb, I figure they're not through with us yet. Mark my words.'

This put Reb into a sour, thoughtful mood and he left Pete, telling him to have a look at some cows and calves in a nearby canyon while he rode on towards the Box S boundary. When cattle grazed on open range it was to be expected that different brands would get mixed. Nobody bothered about this until round-up time when ranchers cut out their own stuff. But this Boulder River range was a different kettle of fish.

Next morning Reb rose early and got the buckboard ready for the journey to town. Sue called him to breakfast and directly afterwards they set out along the fork that linked up with the Hartville road.

All the way Sue chatted merrily and Reb found himself comparing the stricken woman he had found on his arrival at the ranch with the youthful, vivacious girl who sat beside him now. He thrilled when he speculated on how much he had contributed to this change in her.

Above them the sky was blue, with little fluffy clouds drifting before the gentle wind. The late spring sunshine was growing in warmth, and all about them new grass shoots tinted the landscape a deep shade of glistening green.

They reached Hartville around ten o'clock and Sue insisted on Reb leaving the buckboard at the livery and escorting her to a cafe where she said she used to work and where they drank tea and ate tiny pastries. Reb was conscious of the curious stares his appearance with Luke's widow evoked, and he was sweating profusely when

Sue, after dragging him around town with her, told him she wished to visit the dressmaking shop.

'Then you'll not need me around.'

'I won't be long,' she told him. 'Would you take this grocery list and see what you can do with it?'

'Sure thing, ma'am,' he grinned.

Reb watched her as she strode off along the sidewalk and noted the deferential nods and verbal greetings she received. When he finally plucked his gaze from Sue he became aware of more curious glances being slanted at him.

He shouldered through the batwings of the Cowman's Bar and headed slowly to the counter. The bartender whom Talbot had called Fred, and who had refused him a drink, was on duty and he started wiping the counter when Reb entered.

'Howdy, mister. What'll it be?'

Reb blinked at the unexpected civility and ordered a beer. He had been ready to drag Fred over the counter if he had refused to serve him and now he felt a trifle confused and drank his beer in silence. After a few minutes he ordered another beer and decided to push his luck.

'You meet a lot of people who drift into town, I reckon?'

'So?' the other urged. 'I see plenty.'

'The name I'm looking for is Dyke. He's got three pards. A Yance, a Bob and a Mexican called Juarez . . . '

He was surprised at a short outburst of laughter. 'Say, you ain't looking much! Them jiggers are wanted for horse stealing and cattle rustling.'

Reb whistled. 'You don't tell me, Fred. So they have visited town?'

'Mostly when the sheriff's out somewhere on the trail,' the bartender supplied. 'I ain't seen them in months, though.'

'I see.' Reb was disappointed. He grunted his thanks and presently went back to the street.

Sheriff Eli Baker was hitching a horse to the rack in front of his office as Reb passed. 'No more dead men, Scott?'

'How about the nester's hanging? Any news?'

Baker frowned. He shook his head and spat at his feet. He finished tying the horse and mounted the planking. 'I'll get them, never fear.'

He would have left Reb but he asked him to wait. 'Tell me, Sheriff, how did you know there was trouble at the Warner homestead that day?'

Baker's eyes glinted briefly and he scratched his jaw. 'Cowhand told me. Frank and me headed out. You can bet we were surprised to find you there.'

'No idea yet who took a shot at you here in town?'

'Wish I had. Scott, you don't rightly trust me, do you?'

'First off I didn't,' Reb admitted with a slow grin. 'Now I do.'

'Mighty handsome of you!'

Baker went on into his office and Reb went to collect the groceries on his list. He had most of the stuff loaded in the buckboard when Sue appeared at his elbow with a parcel under her arm. 'Did you have a nice time?'

'Passable,' he told her. They had just finished loading the last of the supplies when Dean Talbot, accompanied by a stranger to Reb and Sue, came out of a saloon and began walking along the street towards them. They were almost level with the Box S couple when Talbot raised his head and stared at them. An angry glint came into his eyes as he glanced at Reb before looking directly at Sue. He smiled, inclining his head.

Reb switched his attention to the other man, noting the shifty look on his face and the two guns hanging low at his sides. He had never seen this man before and he wondered with a little chill if this was one of the gunslingers that Talbot was reputed to have hired.

'Well, well, if it isn't Sue!' Talbot greeted briskly. 'And Mr Scott.'

Reb regarded him coolly, conscious of the stranger weighing him up closely.

He heard Sue say: 'Hello, Dean. How are you?'

'Just fine, Sue. I'm glad I've run into you, as there's something I want to discuss with you.'

'She's leaving town right now,' Reb told Talbot. 'If you've anything to discuss with Sue you can call on her at Box S — so long as you call when I'm there.'

'Hey, what kind of talk is this!' Talbot spread his hands in appeal to Sue while he affected a look of disappointment.

Sue laid a hand on Reb's arm but he shook it off gently and took a pace away from her. 'Talbot, it's the only kind of talk you're going to get from this on out,' he informed the rancher in an icy voice. 'And if you're thinking of asking Sue again to marry you, you can forget it, because she's going to marry me.'

8

'Reb!' Sue protested, while high colour stained her cheeks.

'It's true anyhow,' Reb asserted doggedly, his eyes challenging Talbot. 'I reckon it's time we made it plain to everybody.'

Dean Talbot had gone very pale and his mouth trembled slightly. The man at his side sneered openly at Reb and stuck his thumbs into his gunbelt, close to the heavy revolvers.

'You'd better mind how you talk to Mr Talbot, friend,' he said in a gruff voice. 'Else I might have to teach you some manners.'

'Reb,' Sue said quickly, 'get on to the seat and take me home. Do you hear me, Reb? I wish to go home.'

Still Reb stood where he was, his narrowed eyes flitting from the rancher to the stranger with him. He wondered if Talbot would press for a showdown here in town.

'Don't you hear what the lady said?' the stranger demanded, his voice sinking into a slow, insolent drawl. 'Go take her home, boy, and watch you don't fall off her apron strings.'

'Easy, Tex, easy,' Talbot said, making a show of mollifying his companion. 'Mr Scott is all worked up right now, but he'll cool down later, maybe.'

But the man called Tex brushed Talbot aside and faced Reb with bared teeth. 'I don't like the way he talked to you, Mr Talbot, and he's sure going to say he's sorry and he won't do it any more. Right, Scott?'

'Like blazes I will,' Reb spat. 'Sue, take the rig and wait for me at the end of the street.'

'No, Reb. I won't move until you come with me.'

'Sue, get going!' Reb snarled at her, never taking his eyes from the lean man who was now poised like a rattlesnake to strike. 'Talbot, you can call him off now if you want to. If you don't you're going to be real sorry. I mean it.'

'Tex,' Talbot said easily, 'you heard Mr Scott. Maybe you ought to let it sit for now. We can take it up again some other time.'

'It's out of your hands, boss,' Tex cried vibrantly. 'Scott, you apologise for what you just said or *go for your gun*!'

At that instant Sue rushed between them and Reb caught her arm and flung her back against the wheel of the buckboard. She stood then, pale as death, pleading with both men to have sense.

'You going to draw, Scott?'

Reb ran his tongue over his underlip. He knew he had always been fast with a gun, but could he prove the equal of this cold-faced hired killer?'

'You really intend to force this, Tex?'

'*Damn you — draw*!'

The man was going for his pistol when Reb moved. Then his right hand was driving down and sweeping up and two shots boomed out, so closely spaced they seemed to be a single explosion.

Sue screamed. Her gaze flew to Reb's face, a strange, dark mask of awesome intent. Then she looked at the stranger called Tex. It was like a wild nightmare. Tex was standing on his toes and fixing Reb with a terrible stare. A split second he stood thus, then he seemed to lose all co-ordination. His revolver fell from his hand a moment before his knees gave and he crumpled at Reb's feet.

Reb lifted his still-reeking gun to Dean Talbot. He had an urge to blast this man down, also. But something held him back, some warning instinct that told him the time was not yet.

'You planned this, mister,' he grated at the rancher. 'You figured your gunslick would be fast enough to cut me down. Now you can see how good he was. You bought a bad bargain, Dean!'

Talbot just stood, gaunt-featured and staring. A crowd had gathered and formed a circle about them. It broke when Sheriff Eli Baker puffed his way up and looked at the dead man.

'Who is he?' he demanded of Talbot.

'I — I don't know, Eli. I just met him in a saloon. He said he'd a score to settle with a man called Scott. He said he and Scott had fought once.'

'You're a liar!' Reb hissed. 'Sheriff, Talbot is hiring these gunmen to run us small ranchers and hoemen out of the territory.'

'You shot this man, Scott?'

'I did. But he drew first.'

The sheriff swept the crowd with his troubled gaze and when heads nodded in agreement with Reb he scratched his jaw and turned the gunman's body over with his boot.

'All right,' he said grimly. 'Some of you carry him off the street. Scott, you can go, but you'd better watch out. You're a smarter gent than I took you for. And a more dangerous one to boot.'

'I can look after myself, Sheriff,' was the taut reply.

Reb turned to Sue who had scrambled to the seat of the buckboard. He climbed up beside her and took the ribbons out of her hand. 'You can quit trembling, Sue,' he said softly. 'I'm sorry you had to see that, but there was no other way. Now you know what kind of man Dean Talbot is, if you didn't know before.'

He sent the buckboard lurching down the street and when he reached the outskirts of town Sue put her head against his shoulder and began sobbing uncontrollably. Reb brought her into the circle of his arm and marvelled at the great tenderness that stirred in his breast.

★ ★ ★

Overnight, almost, the name of Reb Scott spread to all corners of the range. It seemed that the man he had shot on Saturday in Hartville was Tex Haddock, a gunman with a reputation in Texas as well as Arizona. And when the news went out that Dean Talbot had hired Haddock, sympathy started swinging to the side of the small ranchers and homesteaders that Talbot was seeking to drive from the range.

On Monday, when Reb journeyed to Hartville on an errand for Sue, he was greeted on all sides with a show of respect and friendliness. Reb accepted this change of feeling with characteristic coolness. He knew too well the ways of a crowd. Today he was a good fellow because he had done something that earned their applause; tomorrow, if he failed to cope with another such problem, they would treat him as something lower than a cowhand who had just staked his saddle in a poker game.

Even Sheriff Baker showed a subtle change of face when he ran into him on Main Street. 'Scott, you haven't got any leads on the regulators yet, by any chance?' Baker asked him.

'I'm far too busy at the minute looking after cows to bother with regulators, Sheriff,' Reb responded.

The lawman frowned, scrubbing his chin in the way he had. 'I see. Does this mean you've given up trying to catch the men who hanged your brother?'

'You said he was a rustler,' Reb reminded him. 'So why are you concerned about his killers getting caught?'

'Well, I'm not sure that Luke was a rustler, after all.' Baker plucked thoughtfully at his lip. Then: 'You haven't seen Dean since Saturday?'

'I don't want to see him.'

'Maybe you don't. But I've a hunch you haven't heard the last of him, all the same. Did you ever try to figure out what happened to Milt Forbes the night he turned up at your place with a white hood?'

'I've gone over a lot of angles,' Reb admitted. 'But I'm not really bothered

188

about Milt Forbes, Sheriff. The people I would worry about are people like old Hack Fraser who was murdered because he knew something about the regulators. And Warner, because he wouldn't scare and clear out.'

'And Milt Forbes?' Baker pressed.

'Well, it certainly looks like Forbes was in with the regulators. Maybe he was going to squeal on them too. *Quien sabe*? Come to that, Sheriff, you might know something about them too, like I hinted before.'

Baker swore and Reb wheeled away, chuckling, convinced that the sheriff, whatever his failings, was in no way linked with the cowardly riders who hid behind white masks.

On the way home, Reb wondered about Jim Dyke. If there was not so much work to be done about the ranch he would have taken another trip into the hills. He wondered too what had become of the four men Pete Ferris had followed and who had overpowered, first Pete, and then himself. He thought too of the stranger who had taken a shot at him in the snow. These incidents provided Reb with a lot of questions and it irked him that he could not come up with one satisfactory answer.

* * *

Next day Reb and Pete were on the prowl for mavericks in a brushy canyon at the east end of their range when the sky suddenly became overcast and rain commenced to fall, slowly at first in large drops that bored little holes in the dust, and then in a steady downpour that turned the landscape into a dismal, misty blur. They had their slickers along but the rain grew so heavy that they looked around for shelter. They found refuge from the driving storm in a cave where there was a wide overhang of rock and where the horses could be sheltered also.

Both men were smoking and staring morosely at the hundreds of tiny rivulets that gushed down towards the canyon mouth when presently they heard the snort of a horse. At once they became alert and exchanged puzzled glances. Reb's right hand went under his slicker where it found the worn butt of his gun.

'Somebody pretty close,' Pete Ferris whispered unnecessarily, and Reb signalled him to be silent. He pushed the horses deeper into the cave and then came back to the entrance where he peered along the winding reaches of the canyon.

Four riders were on the move down there, waterlogged hats flopping in the wet wind, shoulders hunched over the necks of their horses. Reb watched as they pushed a small herd of cattle past the canyon mouth and passed from sight behind a cliff ledge.

Pete Ferris' fingers were biting into his arm and he shook the hand off and jerked his head at the stock. 'Get the nags, Pete,' he said tightly. 'It looks like we've happened on a sure enough piece of cow stealing.'

'You reckon it's Dyke and his pards, Reb?'

'I don't know, but we'll soon see. Come on.'

They climbed into slippery wet leather and started down the canyon at a slow, stiff-legged pace where the deep dust was gradually turning into a clinging, muddy mess. When they reached the mouth of the canyon they saw the four men ahead, turning the cattle in a northeasterly direction towards the rain-hazed outline of the timbered hills.

'How do we take them?' Ferris demanded eagerly. 'I vote for shooting the daylights out of them from here.'

'You're crazy! No, Pete, I think we ought to tag behind them until they call a halt. There's four of them, you know, and two of us.'

'Which makes things about even,' Pete grinned.

Reb restrained himself until the men and cattle had passed from sight through a scattering of rocks and high boulders, then he pushed the bay after them at a walk. There was no doubt in his mind that these men had just stolen beef belonging to Box S, and he told himself that this time they would not get away with it.

The trail was easy to follow and wandered in and out through a section of high cliffs and broken boulders. A bright fork of lightning ran through the grey heavens and a shattering roll of thunder broke into the monotonous drum of rain. Reb rounded a weathered rock formation to catch a glimpse of the rustlers just disappearing into the entrance of yet another canyon.

He halted and looked at Ferris whose wet face was tight and eager. The older man gaped in surprise. 'Why drive them into the canyon?' he demanded.

'You never can tell, Pete. Maybe they have a secret hideaway somewhere around here. Let's have a look.'

They slowed as they approached the opening in the fissured rock walls and

Reb took a cautious glance into the canyon. It proved to be no deeper than he had thought and there was no sign of the men or cattle.

Concluding that the rustlers must know of an outlet that would give on to the base of the hills, he proceeded through the brush and mud with Pete trailing him. Now they were in between the lofty walls and Ferris scanned the rugged escarpments. He kept looking behind him, growing nervous and apprehensive. And when Reb suddenly brought his bay to a halt the older man pulled his gun out, seeing what Reb had just seen.

A small herd of ten or twelve cattle was sheltering in the lee of an out-jutting ledge and the Rowel brand was visible on their flanks. Of the men who had been driving them there was no sign. Alarmed, Reb was hauling his horse about when a shout came from behind a rock over on their right.

'We've caught you red-handed, Scott, rustling our beeves!'

'Get out, Pete!' Reb yelled. 'It's a trap.'

Pete Ferris opened fire as he flung himself low on his horse's neck and raced for the mouth of the canyon. Reb followed suit, swinging his sixshooter clear and blasting angrily at the place where the ambushers were holed up.

They were almost at the canyon entrance when guns rattled on either side of it and they had to wheel away to the right. Reb saw a clump of rocks and thorny brush and he headed to it, hearing the bark of pistols and the snarl and whip of lead tearing into the cliffs in front of him. He heard Pete shout and turned to see the man tumbling over his horse's head. The horse made a single attempt to rise but fell back and flopped awkwardly into the mud, dead.

Pete Ferris came bounding up and started to run towards Reb. Reb twisted the bay about and brought it round where the beast would protect Pete from the flying bullets. He reached for Pete as he jumped and hauled him across the bay's neck, then he continued towards the rock clump, sure that they would be blasted down before they could reach it.

Thunder rumbled through the heavens, and the boom of the ambushers' pistols and rifles was drowned out. Lightning flared and danced along the canyon rims and then Reb was reining the bay in among the rocks at the side of the canyon and Pete Ferris was slithering to the ground. Reb dropped from the saddle and gripped the beast's reins, holding it in shelter from the gunfire.

Pete wiped mud from his face and swore hoarsely. 'The dirty coyotes. They've been waiting for a chance to pull a trick like this, Reb. They knew we were out rounding up stray calves and they figured they could get us into this canyon where they could gun us down.'

'Sure.' Reb agreed. 'And then they would get the sheriff out to see the cattle we were supposed to be rustling.

When Baker found us dead and saw Talbot's stock, he would just have to believe their story about trailing us and catching us stealing Rowel beef.'

'I guess we're as good as dead anyhow,' Pete opined. 'They've got us pinned down here so that we can't budge.'

Even as Pete spoke another volley broke out and slugs spattered all about them. When it ceased Reb let loose with his rifle which he had dragged from the saddle boot. He knew there were two of the men at the canyon entrance and that the other two were on the opposite side of the canyon from them. He wondered if Talbot was here himself but he doubted that. Talbot would leave a job like this to men of the stripe of Tim Stanton. He was sure it was Stanton who had shouted at him. Stanton would be only too pleased to get his own back on Reb.

The rain was beating in at them with increased fury and the sky was growing darker with every passing minute. Behind them the walls of the canyon rose up in steep slopes, and it was plain that escape by scaling the cliff face was out of the question. The small herd of cattle was lowing and stamping through the mire, but every time the cattle tried to reach the mouth of the canyon they were driven back by gunfire.

'If we can only stick it out till dusk, Reb, we might have a chance,' Ferris said hopefully.

'They're likely thinking of that too, Pete. My bet is that they'll try to rush us before dark really sets in. Can you see any sign of them?'

Pete peered round the edge of a boulder, blinking against the fine rain. It was as though a grey curtain was being drawn down the centre of the canyon. 'All I can see is rocks where they must be lying. I — ' Pete broke off and ducked as a rifle cracked and pieces of rock flew all about them. He swore as he pulled his sixgun out and triggered.

'They've got our position figured, right enough. If only the two jiggers weren't posted at the mouth of the canyon . . . '

Reb raised a hand as somebody began shouting at them. 'Hey, Scott,' the voice called. 'We're going to give you a chance to come out of there. If you don't — '

Then wind caught the rest of the words and a sullen boom of thunder drowned out all else.

Reb looked grim. 'Do you want to step out there and take a chance on their tender mercies, Pete?'

'I just hope they'll make their rush soon, so I can blast a few of them to Hades,' Pete responded, flashing his teeth.

They settled down to wait and watch. Their eyes smarted as they squinted through the rain. Pete Ferris concentrated on the mouth of the canyon while Reb tried to see across to the opposite side. Minutes passed and no more shots were fired. They became anxious as the evening darkened and still the ambushers failed to make a move. It occurred to Reb that they might have some means of getting behind and above them, but he discounted the notion when he peered up the ragged cliff behind him where water streamed in white, smoke-like torrents.

They became stiff and cramped and Reb's horse was growing more restive as time passed. Now there was no sign of the Rowel cattle at all and Reb began to hope that the men had grown discouraged and moved out of the canyon. Pete wanted to risk leaving their hiding place and make a break for it, but Reb told him to wait a little longer. It would be full dusk shortly and then they would stand a better chance.

The lightning had ceased forking the heavens and the thunder was rolling away to the south. The rain was easing a little but they were cold and miserable, and almost wet through in spite of their slickers. At length the shadows were so thick in the canyon that Reb was sure it would be almost impossible to distinguish shape or form. He clawed the bay's reins with stiff fingers and came erect. 'You climb up first, Pete,' he said and waited until the cowhand obeyed. Then he pushed his rifle into the boot and swung up behind him.

'What happens if they open up as soon as we head out?' Pete wanted to know.

'We'll just keep going for the opening,' Reb told him. 'Ready?'

'Let's go, pard!'

Reb jabbed spurs to the bay and the beast leaped forward. It charged straight into a clump of brush and tore through, and then Reb reined it round towards the canyon mouth. Every second he waited for guns to open up and to feel the smack of a heavy slug. But nothing happened and they emerged from the canyon into safety.

Reb brought his charging bay round

in a wide circle and hauled it in, facing the gloomy entrance to the canyon. He half-expected to see the four riders racing down on them, and when nothing showed he frowned his puzzlement.

'Reb, they got tired of waiting for us to show!' Pete cried. 'They've cleared off home.'

But Reb was not so sure. It would not be like Dean Talbot's men to take so much trouble to corner them and then give up easily. There was more to this, something behind the move that he could not understand.

'I can't figure it, Pete,' he said.

'Reb, don't you see: shooting Tex Haddock has given you a rep that these hellions respect. They've made a show of doing what Talbot likely told them to do. Now they'll go home and say we had a dozen men along and were too many for them.'

'I wish you were right, Pete. But I doubt it.'

His thoughts flitted back to Sue. Sue

alone at the ranch house, defenceless against whatever dark plan Dean Talbot was hatching. He spurred the bay so fiercely that Pete Ferris almost became unseated and demanded to know what the hurry was.

'Pete, don't you see,' Reb hissed over his shoulder. 'This is working out exactly the way Talbot has planned it.'

'What! You mean it was a trick to keep us away from the ranch?' Pete choked and began to swear savagely. 'If that rat has touched a hair of Sue's head I'll — '

He ceased talking as the bay went into a long lope that carried the double burden at a surprising speed over the wet, dismal terrain. Mile after mile fell away behind the horse's hooves, and Reb took chances he would not have taken in broad daylight in normal circumstances. At length they heard the distant song of the river and now Reb turned into the south and soon crossed the stage road.

The first thing he looked for when the dark outline of the ranch loomed up was a light in the window of the main building, and when he broke through some trees and saw the yellow glow he sighed his relief and slowed the panting horse.

'Reb, you've been killing your nag for nothing,' Pete said gustily. 'Sue's here and she's all right.'

'And I bet she's worrying her head off because we're late in getting home,' Reb added with a nervous chuckle.

He put the horse through the gate and drew up in the yard. He waited for Sue to open the door, and when she failed to appear he concluded she was busy with some chore. He dismounted first and let Pete use his shoulder to ease his awkward position on the bay.

'You go in, Reb. I'll turn the horse into the corral.'

Reb thanked him absently. His eyes were on the door of the ranch house and he wondered why Sue did not show. He mounted the porch and shook himself free of the slicker, then he used a damp handkerchief to wipe a wet face and neck. He slapped his hat against the timber wall before lifting the latch of the door and going in.

Yellow lamplight dazzled his eyes before he saw the fair-haired man in the chair by the stove and his hand drove down to his gun. Then another figure moved in behind him from the side of the door and the muzzle of a sixshooter was rammed hard against his ribs.

'Take it easy, Mr Scott,' a sibilant voice hissed, and he swung to look into the face of a Mexican.

Reb divined at once that the man by the stove was none other than Jim Dyke. There could be no mistaking the mop of blond, almost yellow, hair and the low laugh that fell mockingly on his ears. This was one of the men he had glimpsed in the woodland cabin and this was how Sue had described the man wanted by the law.

The bright eyes crinkled up as they

considered Reb. 'So you're the gent that paid us a call in the woods?' Dyke said slowly, savouring the tall man's surprise and concern.

Reb was thinking of Sue as the hard revolver muzzle continued to bore into his side and a dull, throbbing anger built in his breast and threatened to stifle his breathing.

'Where's Sue?' he grated.

The revolver poked so hard that he winced and glared at the man who held it. A wicked sneer grooved deep lines at the corners of the Mexican's mouth.

'Where did you leave your compadre?' Jose Juarez scowled.

'Outside.'

'I know that much, hombre. But where?'

Dyke was starting to speak again when the scrape of Pete Ferris' boots came over the gallery floor. Dyke slid out of his chair and waved the Mexican clear of the door.

'I don't need to warn you, Scott,' he breathed. 'Jose will shoot you if you speak. Then I'll bore your pard before he knows what's happening. I've a score to settle with you, remember.'

Reb had to stand there while the door was pushed open and Pete Ferris entered the room.

9

When Pete saw the Mexican and Dyke his mouth fell open in surprise, then he cursed and took a quick step backwards.

'Hold it,' Dyke yelled at him. 'I'll kill you if you move.'

'Dyke! Damn you, I know you . . . ' Pete's voice trembled.

'And you are the one who shot me in the arm.' The Mexican reached quickly and gripped him by the neck of his shirt. With a strong movement he hurled Pete across the room where he came up hard against a couch. He bent there a minute and Reb guessed what was passing in his mind.

'Take it easy, Pete,' he warned. 'It looks like we've walked into a nest of rattlers.'

Pete faced Jim Dyke then, lips twisted, eyes fiery. 'Where is Mrs

Scott?' he demanded. 'What have you done with her?'

'She's safe enough — for the minute,' Dyke told him. He said to Reb: 'Get over there beside your sidekick.'

Again the Mexican's revolver bit into his ribs and he moved over and stood beside Pete. The smile had left the blond man's face and he pulled out a watch from his vest pocket and consulted it.

'I'm sorry you had to stay out there in the rain for so long,' he said. 'But we needed the time.'

Reb's eyes were narrow slits. 'It was you who ordered the hellions to drive the cattle into that canyon,' he murmured, trying to fit the pieces of the puzzle together so that they might make sense. 'This says you're the gent who rods the crew that goes around with white masks.'

'We gave your brother his chance,' Dyke said carelessly. 'But he wouldn't take it.'

'You asked him to pay you a hundred

a month to protect his stock. But you were really trying to scare him out of here. You are the boss of the regulators, Dyke?'

The blond man's eyes gleamed. 'You're pretty smart, Scott. You know a little and you're anxious to know more.'

'I just want to know the names of the men who strung my brother from a tree,' Reb retorted icily.

The Mexican shrugged. 'What good would it do you now, hombre? You have reached the end of the trail.'

Cold prickles raced up and down Reb's spine. He looked at Pete to see how he was taking this. Pete was glancing at the door leading off the living room and Reb knew he was trying to figure out where they had Sue. His gaze came back to the bright eyes of Jim Dyke. 'Did you hang my brother?' he asked flatly.

'I gave him his chance.' Dyke became brusque. 'Let's cut the gab. Loosen your gunbelts and let them drop. You first, Scott.'

Reb considered him. His eyes lifted to the swarthy face of Juarez who was watching hopefully, gun raised in hand. He knew the man would be pleased to see him make a foolish move so that he could shoot him down.

'I'm getting impatient, Scott.'

Reb sighed raggedly. Very carefully he unbuckled the heavy belt and let it fall to the floor. Dyke gestured at the Mexican who moved swiftly in and brought the belt out with his toe. He carried it to the table.

'Now you.' Dyke gestured to Pete Ferris. 'Quick!'

'Where is Sue?' Reb said. 'If anything — '

'Shut up,' Dyke spat. He waited until Pete had eased his gunbelt to the floor and his companion had dragged it clear, then he said to Jose Juarez: 'Go get the ropes. When you tie them, bring their horses. Hurry, pard.'

The Mexican slipped out of the room and Reb stared at the blond man who now looked sober and grim. 'What do you intend to do with us?' he asked huskily.

'What do you think, mister? What usually happens to a widelooper who gets caught with rustled stock on his hands.'

'But we haven't been rustling anybody's stock, damn it!' Pete exploded. 'If you keep this up, Dyke you're in big trouble.'

'You don't mean you're going to hang us?' Reb demanded incredulously.

Dyke rubbed his nose and sniffed. He seemed a little disconcerted, but he was cold and ruthless, and Reb knew they could expect no mercy from him.

'I do, Scott,' he said flatly. 'Now shut up.'

'But you're making a mistake. You know we haven't stolen anybody's cattle. What kind of dirty trick are you working?'

'Scott, there's about twenty head of Rowel stuff in that new corral you've made.'

'What!'

'Reb, this is the trick they worked on Luke,' Pete Ferris grated. 'They put Luke on a spot and now they're going to do the same thing with you and me. And I'll bet anything that Dean Talbot's behind it.'

The Mexican came in with two strong lariats. He gestured at Pete. 'Lie down on your face.'

'You just go to hell, greaser.'

The Mexican stepped over and slashed his hand across Pete's cheek. 'Lie down,' he snarled.

Reb licked dry lips as he considered Dyke and the gun that was levelled on him. Dyke met his gaze and a small smile tugged at his mouth. 'Maybe you'd rather have a bullet, Scott. But the first one mightn't kill you, and they do say that the rope is plenty quick.'

'Dyke, tell me one thing: where's Sue?'

'She's safe. That's all you're concerned about, I'm sure. It's all you'll have time to be concerned about.'

The Mexican had forced Pete to lie

down on his face. Now he ordered him to put his hands behind his back. A vision came up before Reb of a rope end dangling from a tree limb, and a crude wooden marker that had some words carved on it. With a sudden yell he flung himself forward, diving at Jim Dyke's legs.

Dyke swore and fired. A bullet screamed past Reb's right ear and then he was grappling with Dyke's legs. With a mighty tug he swept the blond man off his feet and once more the gun exploded.

A terrible yell of agony came from Juarez and Reb threw a quick glance to see him holding his stomach where blood was gushing through his fingers in a bright stream. Pete Ferris was shouting and trying to get to his feet. Then Dyke's gun barrel slammed into Reb's shoulder and he rolled, shocked by the pain.

The blond man tried desperately to get out of Reb's reach and Reb swung his boot. It cracked solidly against

Dyke's ankle and the man stumbled and went down. Still he tried to bring his sixgun to bear. Reb shook his head and came erect. He kicked out once more and Dyke's gun went flying from his hand.

Then Reb had the outlaw by the shirt collar and was hauling him upright. When the frightened face came up he swung his right fist and felt a satisfying pain run along his arm. Dyke sagged back against the table, blood oozing from his broken lips. He was coming off it when Reb slammed a straight left into his stomach and sent him reeling to the floor, retching and moaning.

Reb stabbed a look at Pete Ferris. Pete was standing over the Mexican who was bent in two on the floor, whispering feverishly in Spanish. Even as Reb watched, Juarez suddenly stiffened and a choking gurgle died in his throat.

Reb stepped over Dyke and told him to get up. He shouted at Pete to grab his gun and keep it handy, and then he had his fingers in Dyke's shirt front and was hauling him erect.

'Where's Sue?' Reb snarled.

'I — I don't know.'

Reb shook the man fiercely and forced him back against the wall of the room. He waited until the face came up on a level with his own, then he hissed grimly: 'Dyke, I'm going to kill you with my bare hands if you don't tell me.'

'I told you I don't — Aw!'

Reb hit him hard across the mouth. 'Pete, bring my gun.'

'You wouldn't shoot me, Scott!'

Pete handed over the gun while his eyes bored into Dyke. 'Give it to him, Reb,' he said with passion. 'He killed Luke and he thought he had you too.'

Reb pushed the muzzle of the Colt into Dyke's chest. 'Your very last chance to tell me where Sue is.'

Dyke sucked air noisily through his mouth. 'All right,' he croaked. 'Let me go.'

Reb slammed him against the wall and stood back, gun on a level with the man's midriff. 'It'd better be the truth, mister.'

'You know that cabin in the woods . . . ' Dyke blurted out.

Reb and Pete exchanged glances. 'The one you used as a hideout?' Reb queried.

Dyke nodded. 'That's where the woman is.' His eyes sought the body of Jose Juarez and a shiver ran through him.

'Who hanged my brother?' Reb demanded next.

'I don't know, Scott. I don't — ' He broke off as Pete Ferris smashed a fist into his ear. Dyke staggered and threw the lank blond hair from his face.

'Easy, Pete,' Reb warned. 'I'll make him talk, all right. Now, mister, this is your last chance to squeal like a hog. You've about ten seconds to tell me all you know about the regulators and who hanged Luke.'

Dyke rubbed his injured ear. For a

minute he looked sullen, but when the click of Reb's gun being cocked broke in on the silence his shoulders slumped and he threw his arms out in a gesture of despair. 'We had a deal with the regulators,' he began. 'We lifted cattle from any spread they said and drove them to the ranch or homestead of whoever was to be set up for a hemp necktie.'

'You coyote!' Pete Ferris flamed. 'So it was you that brought the Rowel stuff here so Luke could be called a rustler.' He took another step towards Dyke but Reb waved him off.

Reb's features were bleak and there was little mercy in his eyes as he told Dyke to go on talking. 'Why did you offer protection to Luke when you knew he was slated for a rope?'

'That was an idea of our own,' the other replied slowly. 'It's a trick we worked on other ranges until things got too hot for us. We'd offer our services as protectors and if a rancher didn't pay up we came back at night and drove off some of his cattle. Then we'd call again and see if he'd changed his mind about needing protection.'

'Did they pay up then?'

'Sometimes they did. Often they chased us and we had to run for it. We just hit this range last summer. We heard of these regulators and figured we'd better move on in case they caught us lifting stock. But then we found out that the white hoods and the hangings were only an excuse to scare off nesters and small ranchers that were in — a certain gent's way.'

'Whose way?' Reb's voice was as sharp as the crack of a whip.

'I — I can't tell you.'

'You'd better, friend. I think I know his name anyhow.'

'All right, Scott. I reckon you do know. Dean Talbot is the boss of the regulators. He has dreams of running the biggest cattle empire in the west. We made a deal with him to do most of his dirty work, but, so help me, Scott, we never took part in any necktie party. We had nothing to do with your brother's death.'

'No, but you cleared the way for Talbot.'

'Reb, you're forgetting about Sue,' Pete butted in. 'How do we know she's all right?'

'She's all right,' Dyke said quickly. 'Bob Cole and Yance Kibben have her up in that cabin. It was Talbot's idea. He sent men to watch you today and follow you. They had orders to keep you out of the way somehow until the woman could be taken from here. Then he aims to make her marry him.'

'And what was to happen if Sue refused?' Reb urged huskily.

'I don't know, Scott. But you can bet Talbot would work out something when he got rid of you.'

'Sure,' Pete rasped. 'When you had us hanging from the tree where they hung Luke. And you say you're no killer!'

Dyke had no answer to that. He shuddered. He was white of face and looked as if he might be sick at any minute.

'How much was Talbot going to pay you for taking care of us?'

'I don't know. I — I'm not sure.'

'How much?' Reb insisted.

'Five hundred dollars.'

'Why did he shoot Milt Forbes?'

'He told us that Forbes was going to back out of the game. He got Milt to stab an old gent down in town because he had been seen listening at the door of the back room in a saloon. Seems they held meetings there.'

'Hack Fraser,' Reb said musingly. 'So it was Forbes who killed Hack? That means old Hack must have known something about them after all. And then they must have seen him talking to me.'

'Talbot's a slick worker, Scott,' Dyke said. 'He even tried to put the sheriff out of the way. But Milt Forbes made a hash of that. Maybe that's why he killed him.'

'How many men at Rowel?' Reb asked next.'

'I can answer that, Reb,' Pete butted in. 'He holds about ten riders right through the year. But I know a couple of them who sure wouldn't run with any regulators.'

'There were six of them,' Dyke told him, 'including Milt. Look, Scott, I've helped you. I've told you all I know. What say you let me ride out of here, and I promise you that you'll never hear of me again.'

'You'd ride out on your pards?'

'Bob and Yance can take care of themselves.'

'They're guarding Sue at the cabin?'

Dyke nodded. A glimmer of hope shone in his eye. Reb said to Pete: 'Rope him tight, Pete. Keep a close eye on him until I get back.'

Dyke bit his underlip and sweat glistened on his brow. He offered no protest as Pete picked up the Mexican's ropes and told him to sit down on a chair. 'I can tie a gent without pushing his face into the floor,' he said. 'And I want to watch you, mister, so that you can't wriggle out of anything.'

Reb waited until he was sure that Dyke would have no chance of escaping from the strong ropes, then he turned to the door. 'We'll keep him here until I can get in touch with the sheriff,' he said. 'That way Luke's name'll be cleared and Dean Talbot'll be known as a murderer of innocent nesters.'

Pete indicated the body of the Mexican. 'Reb, you going to ask me to keep looking at him?'

Reb dragged the body outside and left it in the barn where he had left Milt Forbes before. He recalled the sheriff's warning about finding dead men and he smiled mirthlessly. Sheriff Baker might soon have more dead men on his hands than his deputy could dig holes for. It was a sour joke but it matched Reb's present mood as he went to the corral and brought out the bay. He scouted round until he found the horses belonging to Jim Dyke and Juarez: They had been hobbled well away from the back of the house and he left them there.

The rain had eased off and the night sky had cleared considerably. Stars twinkled where the clouds broke and there was a chance that the moon might show later.

Once clear of the ranch he tried to fix the direction of the cabin in his mind. It would be hard enough finding the exact point in broad daylight, and it would be much more difficult on a black night such as this.

Riding along he tortured himself with the thought of Sue alone in the cabin with Yance Kibben and Bob Cole. And then another thought presented itself that merely drove him to despair. Might not Dean Talbot himself be at the cabin? And again, had Dyke told him the truth regarding Sue's whereabouts? Was it not possible that his two pards were really somewhere about the ranch and that they would quickly overpower Pete and free their leader?

He sweated, trying to still the many fears that marched through his mind. Of course Dyke had been telling the truth. He must have been telling the truth!

An hour later he was in the forest and making his way through the dripping trees and dank undergrowth, hoping against hope that he would soon find Sue. Overhead, the tall branches formed a canopy that turned the woodland floor into a place of dense darkness, where every step was fraught with danger for both man and horse. Now he realised he had made a mistake in leaving Dyke at the ranch with Pete. He should have taken both of them along and Dyke would have been able to show the way.

It was pure luck that led him to the edge of the glade some time later. He broke out of the trees and saw the starlit sky with the moon lifting over the rim of the forest like a wedge of yellow cheese. And before him stood the cabin where Dyke and his men had made their hideout.

Excitement stirred afresh in Reb and he had to make a conscious effort to still the mad thumping of his heart. Light glimmered from round the edges of the burlap sacking on the windows and he saw the shadowy forms of horses close to the cabin.

Reb looped the bay's reins about a tree branch and lifted his gun from leather. Then he started towards the cabin, moving slowly and pausing every couple of yards to look around him and listen.

When he drew close to the front of the place one of the horses snorted and he halted, praying that the men inside would not be disturbed. After a minute he went on and presently he was beside the front window and trying to see past the edge of the covering. It was impossible to see anything and he moved to the door and stood with an ear close to it. From inside came the murmur of voices.

A wave of relief swept over him. At least the men were here. So Sue must be here also. He tip-toed away until he could see the horses plainly and a small grin wiped some of the bleakness from his face. There were only two animals here. Dyke had been telling the truth after all. Sue must have come here riding double on one of the horses.

At the door of the cabin he eased back the hammer of his Colt. There was only one decisive way of handling this situation and it would call for all the nerve he had. He drew a deep breath and kicked the door with all his might.

The door flew inwards and then Reb was inside the candle-lit cabin. One man leaped up from a stool and tried to get his gun out. Reb squeezed the trigger and the bearded man whom he recognised as the bearded one of Dyke's gang swung round in a crazy circle before falling headlong.

A gun barked on Reb's left and he

flung himself to the floor as he brought his revolver to bear again and triggered frantically. The room rocked with the thunder of gunfire. He saw the second man reel back against the wall, still holding his weapon, a look of surprise and terror on his thin face. Reb shot him again as he tried desperately to lift the gun on a line with him. He watched while the man bent at the knees and sagged down in a heap.

Reb rose then and coughed as the swirling gunsmoke stung his lungs. He looked all about the cabin and his heart dropped when he saw no sign of Sue. 'Sue!' he cried. 'Sue, where are you?'

'Reb! Oh, Reb . . . '

He glanced up to where the ladder disappeared into the blackness of the loft and saw her white face in the candlelight. 'Are you all right?'

'I'm all right, Reb.'

She came down the ladder and he lifted her when she was close enough. She was sobbing and her face was wet with tears. She held on to Reb as if she would never let go. 'Oh, Reb, it was dreadful. They carried me out of the house and put me on a horse. They said Dean Talbot wanted to talk with me. Now — now they're dead . . . '

'It was the only way,' he comforted. 'I had to shoot them or they would have shot me. Look, try and pull yourself together before somebody arrives. The sound of the shots will carry through the woods.'

'Oh, yes! Get me away from here, Reb. Please. They told me I could sleep in the loft, but I just lay and cried. Then I heard you come in. And the shooting . . . '

She trembled violently and Reb held her tightly, patting her shoulders. Then he gripped her arm. 'Come on, Sue. Let's get out of here. It's a long ride back to the ranch and I'm not at all sure I'll be able to find the way.'

He pushed her through the door and took a final look at the bodies of the two men. A fire glowed fitfully in the stove and the candle on the table flickered in the draught from the door. He went back and blew out the flame and then he was beside Sue in the wet grass and heading for his horse.

'You can ride my bronc,' he said. 'I'll hunt around for a saddle for one of the other mounts.'

'Reb, couldn't your horse carry both of us? I'm not sure that I could ride just now. I feel so shaky.'

'Whatever you say, Sue,' he told her. 'I just hope we can find our way out of the woods.'

'I don't care where we go, Reb, just as long as you don't let me out of your sight.'

He gripped her shoulders tightly and looked down into her face. It was like a white flower in the faint starlight and his hands moved to her cheeks, feeling how cold they were now.

'I won't ever let you out of my sight, honey. It's one thing you can depend on.'

He lifted her on to the horse and climbed up behind her. He kneed the bay out of the glade and into the darkness of the trees. He knew now what he must do and he vowed that nothing would hold him back.

★ ★ ★

Dean Talbot and Tim Stanton rode away from the Rowel buildings at dawn. They cut across the southeastern fringe of Rowel grazing lands and entered the fringe of the woods as the first streamers of silver and crimson flared out across the sky.

Talbot's face was set and thoughtful as he pushed his chestnut into the pines and he discouraged Stanton's attempts to start a conversation. He had not slept much last night, thinking about Reb Scott and Sue, and Sue's other rider, Pete Ferris. According to his men who had managed to box the two in a canyon yesterday, Scott and Ferris had headed straight home when they left the canyon. Dyke and the Mexican Juarez would have taken care of them

231

by now, and they would be swinging by their necks from those trees where Luke had been hung.

Talbot recalled that he had slept little on the night they had taken Luke out of his house and put a rope about his neck. Maybe there was a soft spot in him somewhere, but he would have to steel himself. Empires were not won by weak-hearted men who balked at the smell of blood or the look of death. He would have to harden his heart and ride over whatever opposition he encountered.

His thoughts moved from Scott and Ferris to Sue alone in the cabin with Kibben and Cole. Dyke had recommended the pair for the job and Talbot hoped he could trust Dyke's judgement. Sue was a very pretty woman and it was just possible that those two might get ideas of their own . . .

He pushed this picture out of his mind too, and thought of Sue when she would be his wife. True, it might take some time for her to forget the Scotts but he was certain that Sue would eventually come to trust him and love him. Had he not almost won her before Luke Scott came along to spoil his chances? If Luke had left Sue alone he might have saved some lives — including his own.

Talbot's mood brightened as he rode through the trees with Stanton close by. In a very short time he would be having his first real sip of success.

10

When the pair were only half a mile or so from the cabin Talbot pulled in to put a cigar between his teeth and strike a match to light it. 'Remember, Tim,' he said, 'we can't afford to make any mistakes now.'

'You figure it's best to get Yance and Bob out of the way?' Stanton wanted to know.

'I told you our plans,' the rancher responded thinly, kneeing his mount along. 'If these gents are allowed to ride off they'll only come back to ask for more money.'

'And Dyke and Juarez, boss? You told them to stay at Box S until you got there.'

'Don't worry. I'll tell him that his two men headed for Hartville,' Talbot said. 'Then he'll only have to share with Jose.'

'You don't intend to have anyone left around who can point a finger at you, do you, Dean?' Stanton's tone carried an inflexion that caused the rancher to frown.

'Something on your mind, Tim?'

'Nothing much. I was just thinking about Milt.'

Talbot bit into the cigar. 'You just think about yourself, Tim. That's the healthiest idea.'

'I reckon I understand you, boss.' Stanton spurred his horse and began to whistle shrilly.

When they broke into the glade where the cabin stood Talbot looked first at the chimney pipe and scowled. 'They're still asleep.'

'You just hope! Maybe they've cleared out. And they might have — '

'I see their horses,' Talbot interrupted him, his voice ragged with relief. 'Now remember what I said. I'll take Sue out of the cabin. Then I'll call Yance outside. That'll be your chance to take Bob.'

'And when Yance comes rushing back into the cabin I'll shoot him too?' Stanton grinned crookedly.

'You've got it, pard.'

'Sure. Then you'll tell Sue that they planned to take her away with them, and that I had to shoot them to protect everybody.'

'You're a real bright fella, Tim,' Talbot applauded. 'Let's open the ball.'

They rode up before the cabin door and Talbot shouted: 'Hey, are you men going to sleep all day?'

He sat then, flinging his cigar stub from him. Nothing stirred from the cabin and he turned a taut face to Tim Stanton. 'What do you reckon?'

'They've cleared out, like I told you. I bet they grabbed the woman and — '

'Blazes, their horses are here!'

Talbot slipped from his saddle, running a finger along his well-shaven jawline. He was really worried. He brought his revolver from its holster and went to the cabin door. He kicked it open and tensed with the gun raised. The door crashed inwards and the Rowel boss stepped through the opening. When he saw the bodies of Yance Kibben and Bob Cole he screwed up his ashen face. 'Somebody has bored them, Tim!'

Stanton almost fell from his horse in his eagerness to get into the cabin. He came up short, swearing softly. 'Dean, I reckon this is Reb Scott's handiwork.'

Talbot pulled air through his teeth as he explored the room. He grasped the ladder and stared up at the loft. He scarcely recognised his own voice. 'Anybody up there?'

He stood back then, sweat beading on his forehead, and ordered Stanton to go up and check the loft. The gunhand shrugged and climbed the ladder. He vanished for a few moments and then reappeared. He shook his head mutely. Next, Stanton went over to the body of Yance Kibben and touched the stubbled cheek. He grimaced.

'I'd say this happened last night,' he

announced then.

'You think Scott really has been here, Tim?' Fear was creeping along the rancher's spine, chilling him to the marrow.

'It all figures, boss. Sue's gone and the gents who were supposed to be watching her are dead. At least somebody has saved me a heap of trouble.'

Talbot stared distastefully at the dead men, then swung to the cabin door, Stanton on his heels. The sun was lifting in the east and long lances of golden light slashed through the trees as the rancher toed into a stirrup iron and nudged his horse. Stanton mounted also and pushed his mount after the big man.

'What you aiming to do, Dean?'

'Head for Box S,' Talbot announced decisively. 'I want to find out what happened to Dyke and Juarez. If Scott has been here in the woods it means he must have gotten away from Jim.'

Stanton let his mind dwell on the

two dead men back there in the cabin and recalled the account he had heard of Reb Scott beating Tex Haddock to the draw in Hartville. He tried to repress a shudder. 'If that's so, then Scott'll be on the warpath for sure,' he declared.

★ ★ ★

Pete Ferris blinked against the glare of the early sun and gazed through the window at the distant road fork for the hundredth time. Behind him in the ranch living room Sue emitted a little sigh.

'I hope Reb won't stay long in town,' she said. 'Pete, do you really think he'll come straight home when he hands Dyke over to the sheriff?'

'I guess he will,' Pete assured her. 'As soon as Dyke tells Eli Baker all he knows about Dean Talbot, Reb will come home. The sheriff will just have to take Talbot in and charge him with murder.'

'Pete, I never knew a man could be so vile, who could stoop so low to gain his ends.'

Pete Ferris shrugged. 'You haven't met too many of Talbot's stripe,' he said wryly. 'I can hardly believe you were going to marry him one time.'

'Please don't remind me, Pete! Luke was worth a dozen Dean Talbots.'

'And his brother, ma'am: how do you rate him?'

Sue blushed as the cowhand chuckled. 'Need you ask? Here, come away from that window and I'll watch for a spell.'

'Don't worry. Reb gave me orders, and I reckon I'll have to carry them out. Unless I'm mistaken, Mr Talbot will soon turn up at the cabin, looking for his future bride. And when he sees that you've gone and finds the gents that Reb Scott — ' Pete stopped speaking, his eyes narrowing on the trail out yonder.

'Do you see something?'

'Two riders coming off the fork,' Ferris said flatly. 'Stay well away from the window and leave this to me.'

Pete levered a shell into the breech of his rifle and raised the weapon to shoulder level. He glanced along the sights and followed the riders as they came on towards the ranch house. He soon recognised the taller of the two newcomers and his heart skipped a beat when he realised this was Dean Talbot.

Sue had gone from the room and now she returned with another rifle, Pete waved her back but she went down on one knee at the window and peered out. 'I've the right to protect my own house, Pete. Who is it?'

'Talbot.'

That silenced the woman and they waited while the riders came on to the yard gate. When they were about to pass under the sign Pete Ferris squeezed the trigger of his Winchester and a piece of wood splintered from the fence, close to the arrivals. They hauled up at once.

'Scott, is that you? Hold your fire!'

'That's Talbot,' Pete hissed. 'This is a chance to shoot him down. Say the word, Sue.'

'Oh, Pete, what can we do — ' The woman had gone very white and her lips trembled. Pete wheeled back to the window.

'What do you want, Talbot?' he shouted.

'That you, Ferris? I want to speak to Scott.'

'He ain't here.'

'Where is he? Let me come in, Pete. Is Sue there?'

Pete rubbed his nose with the back of his hand. He shifted the rifle sight a fraction and triggered once more. Dean Talbot almost tumbled from the saddle of his prancing horse. Tim Stanton pulled his mount round and sent it back through the gate. Talbot screamed at him and shook his fist at the house. He regained control of his horse and sent it after Stanton. At the gate the rancher paused and Pete's third rifle bullet smashed into a fence post and sent wood flying through the air.

'That ain't bad shooting, Talbot,' he yelled above the melee. 'And it's the only warning you can expect, mister. Next shot will drill you plumb centre!'

Tim Stanton had stopped and pulled his rifle from the saddle boot. He was raising it when Talbot gestured angrily and the other reluctantly replaced the weapon. Talbot sent his chestnut pounding after Stanton. The gunman presently drew up and glared at the rancher.

'I don't take that from anybody, boss. Ain't you going to stay and blast them?'

'Scott isn't there,' was the curt response. 'Ferris has been told to mind the house. Likely Sue's there as well.'

'What about Dyke and Juarez?'

'They must have slipped up,' Talbot grated. 'It just shows you that you can't trust anybody. Likely Dyke's in town right now, telling everything to the law to save his own skin . . . '

They continued riding off under the watchful eye of Pete Ferris. Pete remained at the window until the two riders had left the fork where it joined the Hartville road. Then he croaked a nervous laugh and rose to his feet. He partly regretted letting Dean Talbot and his man ride away like that. It was the first time he had had the rancher under his sights, and he felt he would never get a similar opportunity.

'Have they gone, Pete?'

'They've gone,' he told Sue. 'But I'd sooner trust a snake than trust Talbot. He knows Reb ain't here and he's pretty certain that Dyke isn't here either. There's only one good move he can make now to save his hide.'

'What do you mean, Pete?'

'Head to town and try to talk himself off the spot Dyke's story will put him on. And I wouldn't like to bet that he won't be able to do it!'

★ ★ ★

244

It was early when Reb Scott rode into the main street of Hartville with Jim Dyke. Dyke sat his horse with his arms roped behind his back and the long journey had not been a comfortable one for him.

A man came to a store doorway to stare at them, and still another curious cowhand stepped into the road for a closer look. 'Well, I do declare!'

'Keep moving, waddy,' Reb told him.

'Say, ain't that Jim Dyke, the rustler?'

'I'll tell you when I find out.'

Reb had no need to rap up the sheriff this morning. Baker came to the door as Reb brought his bay in at the broken hitchrail. He gaped from Dyke to Reb and ran his fingers through his hair.

'Scott, what's all this?'

Reb slid from his horse without answering. He gripped Dyke by the arm and eased him to the ground. Then he pushed him towards the lawman who took a quick step backwards. Baker went into his office and Dyke heavy-footed in behind him. When the three of them were inside Reb kicked the door shut on a ring of curious faces.

Eli Baker wiped his neck with a kerchief and pushed his hat to the back of his head. He sank down on to his chair behind the ancient desk and tried to speak assertively. 'What's this all about, Scott?'

'Get a pen and paper,' Reb ordered him. 'This gent is just about busting to tell you what he knows about the hell-raising and the hellions. Hooded riders too, you bet.'

'Blazes!'

Dyke made a last throw of the dice. 'Sheriff, you'd better hear the straight of this. This gent just held me up and told me he was going to bring me in. I don't know a damn what it's all — '

Reb was beside him in one stride and his hand cracked against Dyke's jaw with stunning force. The outlaw toppled out of the chair, and before Eli Baker could intervene, Reb dragged him upright and smashed his fist into his face again. Dyke begged him to stop. 'All right!' he cried. 'All right: I'll talk.'

'Get the paper and pen,' Reb snapped at the sheriff. 'And you'd better hurry it up, Eli, because I haven't much time to spare.'

Baker frowned darkly but he obediently poked about in a drawer of his desk and extracted sheets of paper. He brought his quill pen to hand. 'What the blue hell is all this about?' he growled.

'The hooded riders and their boss,' Reb supplied. 'And when Dyke here tells you all he knows, I'm going after Dean Talbot and I'm not going to stop until I rip his dirty game to pieces.'

Baker flung a hard stare at him. 'You're sure Talbot is the gent you want?'

'You just bet, Sheriff. Ask Dyke.'

'What do you say, you sonofabitch?'

The blond man nodded heavily. 'Take this rope off'n my wrists.'

'When you've answered my questions,'

Reb told him. 'You write it all down, Sheriff.'

A short while later Eli Baker was studying Jim Dyke's confession. He looked grim and determined now, like a man whose hopes had begun to achieve realisation. 'All right, Scott. I'll put this bird in a cage and go bring in Talbot.'

Reb looked keenly at him. 'You're really game to go after him, Eli?'

'I said so, didn't I? Scott, I had to be sure of my ground. You must understand how it is. Talbot has men, money, plenty of influence. Come on, hombre,' he said to Jim Dyke, heaving him towards the cell block. 'At least you'll be out of the way for a while.'

Baker had just finished locking Dyke in a cell when his deputy, Frank Kane, came in from the street. His gaze stabbed at Reb before resting on the sheriff. 'I hear you got Jim Dyke.'

Baker gestured to the cells. 'He's in there, Frank. Watch him real good, will you. And don't let anybody in here to see him. You hear me, Frank?'

'I hear you, Sheriff. Where you headed?'

'Going after Dean Talbot. I've just found out for sure that he's the leader of the regulators.'

'Well, what about that! Happens you won't have to go far to look for Talbot. I watched him go into the Cowman's Bar with Tim Stanton and a couple of other Rowel men.'

Reb was making for the door when the sheriff grabbed his shoulder. 'Don't go charging like a crazy loon,' he warned. 'Remember, that saloon is Rowel territory.'

Reb shook the hand off and went into the street. The town was bustling now with people coming and going, and horses stood at most of the hitchracks along the street. Reb slanted his hat slightly over his forehead and started walking towards the Cowman's Bar. Before he reached the doors of the saloon Eli Baker caught up with him, warning Reb to watch his step.

'Get this straight, friend. I want Talbot alive so he can stand trial.'

'That's so? I reckon Talbot's the sort that'll not take kindly to being arrested, Eli,' Reb returned curtly.

He shouldered into the saloon, alert and wary, his eyes flickering over the gathering. There was no sign of Dean Talbot or Tim Stanton but when he looked at the counter he saw the bartender staring at him. Then he hurried to the end of the counter and disappeared through an inner door. He was back by the time Reb and the sheriff reached the bar.

'Tell him to come out,' Reb ordered quietly.

'Who — ' the bartender started to bluster, but the gleam in Reb's eye warned him to break off. He tossed a glance at the door of the back room and a look of relief came to his face when two men came out and sauntered to the counter.

'Kells and Graham,' the sheriff said at Reb's neck. 'Two of Rowel's toughest riders, and likely two of the regulators . . . '

Baker stopped talking as the pair came on to where he and Reb were standing. Baker moved closer to Reb but one of the men eased in between them and the other stopped on Reb's right, so close that it was plain he intended crowding Reb. He was tall, heavy in the chest and shoulders, with blunt, stubbled jawline.

'You're Scott?' he said.

'What of it?'

'I'd like to have a word with you, Mr Scott — outside.'

Reb sensed rather than saw the man's hand sliding down his thigh. With a grunt he swung his arm and his elbow crashed into the man's face. He shouted as he fell back and Reb sprang clear of the counter. His own gun cleared leather as the Rowel man drew and triggered. A bottle exploded behind the bar and Reb's first shot caught the big fellow squarely in the chest, just below the neck. Reb whirled about to where Eli Baker was grappling with the other Rowel man. People were stampeding towards the street and the bartender was peeping fearfully over the counter.

A revolver blasted and Reb saw the sheriff go slack as a trickle of crimson ran down his arm. The second Rowel man was lifting his gun for another shot when Reb brought the barrel of his Colt crashing down on his head. He fell to the floor with a groan. Then Reb turned to the door at the end of the counter. The bartender came out now, a derringer in his hand.

'You can't go in there!' he shouted.

'Get out of my way, damn you,' Reb snarled and kicked at the door of the room.

The bartender was about to shoot at Reb when the sheriff slammed into him and sent him flying. Baker saw Reb burst into the back room and then he heard a savage curse as two guns cracked wickedly. When he got to the door he saw Tim Stanton tottering towards a table for support. Reb, grim and ruthless, swept his revolver over the otherwise empty room.

'Where's Talbot?' Reb demanded of Stanton.

The gunman was clasping his stomach where red stain was oozing from his shirt. He looked sick and ready to drop. He eased himself down, face on the table.

'Window . . . The rat tried to . . . '

Reb's eyes swivelled to the window of the room. Two steps took him over the floor and he hauled the curtains back to see that the window was open half way. Before the sheriff could restrain him, Reb was through the opening and standing on a stretch of waste ground. His gaze caught a man's legs disappearing round a corner at the rear of the main building.

Gritting his teeth, Reb hunted about for an avenue that would take him to the street. He saw an alley mouth and sprinted into it, spur rowels spinning, trying to pick his way across the uneven ground. When he reached the street he was just in time to see a horseman pounding for the south end of town. He glanced up to where his bay stood at the sheriff's office, undecided. There were other horses racked close at hand but he needed a mount right now that he could depend on.

He began running towards the bay, keeping to the firm planking, and knocking people out of his way as he went. In another minute he was pulling the reins loose from the rail and flinging himself into the saddle. He swept down the road again as Sheriff Baker emerged from the saloon, nursing his wounded arm.

'Hold on, Scott,' he called. 'I want to go with you.'

Reb paid no heed. He goaded the bay to the end of the street, and then he paused a moment to peer about him. A cry left his lips when he saw a rider pounding across a level stretch to the north of the stage road, and he sent the bay into a gallop, determined to catch Dean Talbot before he could reach the woods.

Mile after mile sped past beneath flying hooves. Talbot was well-mounted and he rode superbly, and Reb saw that it was not going to be easy overtaking him. The land began to lift and a stretch of timber was visible ahead. He saw that Talbot planned to ride into the woods and lose his trail in the rough country that lay above the trees. Here the bay slowed considerably and Reb became aware of the scorching power of the sun. A half hour later he came in view of a mesa and halted. There was no sign of Talbot and he drew a deep breath through clenched teeth, searching all about him.

He was scanning the rough ground for hoofprints when a sharp crack cut through the high air and a puff of smoke rose behind a cluster of rocks. The bullet scythed through a clump of matted brush and Reb's revolver was blazing viciously before the echoes of the first shot had died. He was surprised to see the figure of a man lift up over the rocks, stagger, and then fall forward.

Without pausing to consider the danger, Reb pressed the bay towards the rocks, and when he drew closer he saw Dean Talbot on his knees, striving mightily to push himself to his feet.

'Get up,' Reb ordered coldly.

'I — I can't — ' He appeared to lose all strength and fell in a heap, swearing and groaning.

Reb slipped from his saddle, pushing his revolver away. He approached Talbot alertly. 'Where are you hit?' The rancher brought a pale face up and Reb saw the blood on his shoulder. 'Get to your feet,' Reb ordered.

'I can't.'

'You've just got a shoulder graze,' Reb grated. He stood back while the rancher struggled to his feet. Talbot was suffering more from shock than from the actual wound.

'What are you going to do with me?'

'Shuck your gun and get on to your horse,' Reb told him. He watched while the other mounted, then: 'Head for the trees.'

'What are you going to do with me?'

'String you up,' Reb said bleakly. 'The way you strung innocent men.'

'No — no!'

'Get going.'

On the crest of a wooded ridge Reb made him dismount and Talbot watched with a terrible fascination while Reb tossed a lariat up and over a stout tree branch. When the loop came down Reb told Talbot to come closer.

'No, Scott,' the big man pleaded. 'Please don't. I'll give you all — '

'Quit squealing,' Reb snapped. He had his gun trained on the rancher when Sheriff Baker and another rider cleared a rise and came towards them.

'Hold it, Scott!' Baker shouted.

It was the instant Dean Talbot chose to make a break for it. With a low cry he scrambled into his saddle, and Reb had no hesitation about triggering his Colt. Talbot tried to mouth something, choked, and fell to the ground.

Eli Baker dismounted and went over to the rancher. 'He's dead,' he announced. 'You were going to hang him, Scott,' he accused flintily.

'That's what I aimed to do.' Reb brought his lariat down and began coiling the rope. He moved with slow deliberation to the bay and levered himself aboard. He grinned crookedly at the sheriff and his companion from town. 'I'm kind of glad I didn't get to hanging him, though. Well, Sheriff, I'll be seeing you around if you need me. I'd better go tell Sue she can sleep without worrying about the regulators. Adios, Eli!'

Baker and the townsman gazed after the tall rider until he had crested a ridge and gone from their view.

We do hope that you have enjoyed reading this large print book.

Did you know that all of our titles are available for purchase?

We publish a wide range of high quality large print books including:
Romances, Mysteries, Classics
General Fiction
Non Fiction and Westerns

Special interest titles available in large print are:
The Little Oxford Dictionary
Music Book, Song Book
Hymn Book, Service Book

Also available from us courtesy of Oxford University Press:
Young Readers' Dictionary
(large print edition)
Young Readers' Thesaurus
(large print edition)

For further information or a free brochure, please contact us at:
Ulverscroft Large Print Books Ltd.,
The Green, Bradgate Road, Anstey,
Leicester, LE7 7FU, England.
Tel: (00 44) 0116 236 4325
Fax: (00 44) 0116 234 0205

Other titles in the
Linford Western Library:

A LAND TO DIE FOR

Tyler Hatch

There were two big ranches in the valley: Box T and Flag. Ben Tanner's Box T was the larger and he ran things his way. Wes Flag seemed content to play second fiddle to Tanner — until he married Shirley. But the trouble hit the valley and soon everyone was involved. Now it was all down to Tanner's loyal ramrod, Jesse McCord. He had to face some tough decisions if he was to bring peace to the troubled range — and come out alive.

THE SAN PEDRO RING

Elliot Conway

US Marshal Luther Killeen is working undercover as a Texan pistolero in Tucson to find proof that the San Pedro Ring, an Arizona trading and freighting business concern, is supplying arms to the bronco Apache in the territory. But the fat is truly in the fire when his real identity is discovered. Clelland Singer, the ruthless boss of the Ring, hires a professional killer, part-Sioux Louis Merlain, to hunt down Luther. Now it is a case of kill or be killed.

GOING STRAIGHT IN FRISBEE

Marshall Grover

Max and Newt were small-time thieves, a couple of unknowns, until the crazy accident that won them a reputation and a chance to reform. But going straight in a town like Frisbee was not so easy. Two tough Texans were wise to them and, when gold was discovered in that region, Frisbee boomed and a rogue-pack moved in to prey on prospectors. In the cold light of dawn, the no-accounts marched forth to die.

TRAIL OF THE CIRCLE STAR

Lee Martin

Finding his cousin, friend, and mentor, Marshal Bob Harrington, hanging dead from a cottonwood tree is a cruel blow for Deputy U.S. Marshal Hank Darringer. He'd like nothing better than to exact a bitter and swift revenge, but as a lawman he knows he must haul the murderers to justice — legally. But seeking justice is tougher than obstructing it in Prospect, Colorado. Hank has to keep one hand on his gun and one eye on his back.

McKINNEY'S REVENGE

Mike Stotter

When ranch-hand Thadius McKinney finds his newly-wedded wife in the arms of his boss, the powerful, land-hungry Aaron Wyatt, something inside him snaps. Two gunblasts later, McKinney is forced to flee into the night with the beef-baron's thugs hot on his trail, baying for his blood. A man cannot run forever, and even when his back-trail is littered with bodies, the fighting isn't over. McKinney decides it is time for Wyatt to pay the Devil.